I0533863

The Church of Latter-Day Eugenics

Chris Kelso & Tom Bradley

Illustrated by Nick Patterson

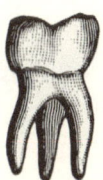

Bizarro Pulp Press
an imprint of JournalStone Publishing

Copyright © 2017 by Chris Kelso and Tom Bradley
Illustrations © 2017 Nick Patterson

Bizarro Pulp Press books may be ordered through booksellers or by contacting:

Bizarro Pulp Press, a JournalStone imprint
    www.BizarroPulpPress.com

    ISBN: 978-1-947654-15-0

Printed in the United States of America
JournalStone rev. date: December 6, 2017

    Cover Art: Nick Patterson

    Interior Formatting: Lori Michelle
        www.theauthorsalley.com

Praise for The Church of Latter-Day Eugenics

Perverse and profane,
Kelso and Bradley make it rain,
sluicing the godly
and fluids (bodily)
down the drain.

—John Skipp,
author of *The Last Goddam Hollywood Movie*

There are sins that men commit for which they cannot receive forgiveness in this world, nor in that which is to come. And if they had their eyes open to see their true condition, they would be willing to have their blood spilt upon the ground, that the smoke thereof might ascend to heaven as an offering . . . and this incense would atone.

—Brigham Young

I had no idea these missionaries came sniffing around hotel rooms. Everyone's seen them, two by two, in identical thin black ties, riding one-speed bikes into residential neighborhoods, knocking on doors. But, here they are, lurking in the corridor of this two-star Hackney flop house. Regulation-issue Mormon underwear glows strangely under the rayon of their matching white shirts, little magic schematics embroidered here and there.

Cheryl, my junior assistant-intern-schlep-pain-in-the-arse, answers the door while I hold down the edge of the bed. She's also surprised to see these two young—er—let's call them *individuals*, for lack of a more accurate term.

"Didja know the Kingdom o' *Gaw-w-wd* has been *ee*-stablished on *Ear-r-r-rth*?" they say in unison, in that far-western USA accent, half cowboy, half swisher. Their voices are too high.

"Look what we have here," Cheryl shrieks. "Which one's Martha, and which one's Arthur?"

"Ease up the homophobia, love," I admonish her. "Just because you want to shag every bloke in the greater London area, it doesn't mean you should do a hate crime on the few who'd rather not. To be honest, I admire their taste."

"*Shag*? How old did you say you were, Fulton?"

Cheryl has no respect for me, the boss, the brains behind this operation.

Our charming lass is just as disappointed as I am in our intruders. I thought the knock on the door was room service bringing me my full English breckie.

Normally Mormon missionaries are strapping young men, something Cheryl would come onto with all her scrawny might, especially this time of day. She's a child of the morning, our Cheryl—

I

or so I've heard. But these two are oddly soft around the edges. Something like those newfangled hermaphrodite Christs you see on crosses in churches lately, the ones who've worked their right hand free of its nail, and reach down to give you a limp high five.

These boys come all the way across the big puddle from the shores of the Great Salt Lake, landing at Heathrow with their well-scrubbed, wide-open faces and little-boy social skills. They roll into one of our slums, and in two minutes flat, the verbal acrobats of our working class have them tied in brain-knots. The whole shabby street is out on their front stoops, jeering, with nary a single new Mormon made among the mob.

As a matter of fact, I kind of feel sorry for the laddies. But not Cheryl. She's lit up a cigarette and is blowing thunderheads of forbidden smoke in their faces, and bellowing—

"You cunts have been drinking too much of that colonial milk from estrogen-overdosed cows!"

She sprays a few pints of aerosol venom, throwing out phrases that include the word *smegma*, which I don't care to repeat, thank you. She grabs the Gideon's Bible from the bedside table, jostling my morning cocktail, and flings it in their faces.

"Try preaching from the real thing, instead of that bleeding *Book of Morons!*"

As if our little heathen's ever read Holy Scripture, apart from the bit where the nice Jewish girl hammers a tent peg into the skull of the poor sod who made the mistake of falling asleep in her presence—as I've recently done.

As the twin Mo-Mos turn to retreat, the room service waiter, wearing an organ grinder's monkey jacket that has seen better days, shoves past them with my yummies, plus whatever muck my Girl Friday has ordered. On the way back into the brownish grayness of the corridor, one of the missionaries reaches into the black dacron polyester pocket on his weirdly rounded hip. He removes a small packet of blue powder and dumps it quickly into the teapot that always comes uninvited on room service carts. (As if I would ever drink something with such a high water content.) This is done in what his sun-blasted brain obviously considers a subtle way, but neither Cheryl nor I miss it.

"What the fuck?" she says, once they're gone.

2

"My feelings, exactly. When you pour it in the loo, don't let a drop of that splash on your fingers. We tabloid journalists learn to be leery of assassination attempts."

"That's one way to make yourself feel important."

"I suppose that sky-colored date-rape drug is intended for *you*, Miss Cub-Reporter-Never-Had-a-Byline-Sub-Trainee-Step-and-Fetch—"

She interrupts my catalogue with, "Piss off, Fulton."

I reckon the General Authorities of the Church of Jesus Christ of Latter-Day Saints read the libel I published last year in *The Prattler*. They sent those young 'uns halfway across the planet to dose me with ricin or something. Anyway, who cares? The full English has arrived in front of me—finally!

"Fuck the Kingdom of Heaven!"

I skewer a black hunk of square sausage onto my fork, swim it around in some runny yolk and thrust it in my mouth, to the evident disgust of Cheryl. She's pretty uptight is young Cheryl. That'll have to change. If she's going to survive in this industry of arrant bullshit and deception the girl will need to seriously man up. I tell her this all the time in fact. I tell her again.

"You'll seriously need to man up Cheryl darlin'."

She gives me this contemptuous glare as she stands aside to let the waiter exit our room. He retrieves the Gid-Bib from the so-called "carpet" and hands it back to her.

"Bit of a wimpy throwing arm there, dearie."

I scoff at Cheryl's anorexic weakness just to remind her of the order of the food chain here. We just covered the trial of Ennis Straker, a charming serial killer who ate the brains of his victims to achieve a sense of immortality. He got an eight year sentence, seemed remorseful enough, and I've met much worse in *The Prattler* staffroom, but poor young Cheryl was thoroughly freaked out by the whole case.

"You getting the lamb brain?" I ask her, as she lifts the cover off her morning meal.

"Eugh, I heard that weirdo in court say brains taste like over-salted scrambled egg."

"I know, but they're good for you."

Cheryl picks away at her Waldorf salad like an archaeologist

4

probing the Earth in search of the next Rosetta Stone. I tell her to get it down her neck, that this is a two-star Hackney hotel, so relax and enjoy for christsakes! She just looks at me all skinny and daft and tightly wound. We proceed to eat in silence. Women have always baffled me.

We're hot on the trail of Bryan Fix, some reality TV knob who escaped from the set of XTV's Celebrity Crack Den. After six weeks of consecutive nominations to keep him IN the den, it seemed the public had spoken. They *really* enjoyed this cunt's descent into drug saturated madness and, I'm sure, were chomping at the bit to bear witness to the UK's first on-screen drug-related suicide. Fair do's. I've got no moral objection to some twat with a quiff offing himself on live television. Doubt we lost a cancer cure. As you can imagine, Fix was, by the end of his stint on Celebrity Crack Den, completely strung out to crack. He can't have gotten far as a disorientated, starving junky on the streets of Greater London, no way.

Time to hit the loo, situated conveniently three feet away from the clanking bed we have been sharing so chastely. (Downright luxuriant budget we get from *The Prattler*.) My full English bursts out of the old baked plum like an Aztec sacrifice. Cheryl is playing around on her mobile phone. I shout from the bathroom—*Oi, you better be brushing up on yer shorthand, luv!*—to which I receive no reply. She's probably texting some ponce with a Corsa.

On the pan, I start thinking about Bryan Fix. He must be nearby. A slew of ex-girlfriends have him sited in Shoreditch or thereabouts as recently as Tuesday. *The Prattler* has been gasping strange rumors of his facial skin being razor-carved an inch deep with creepy secret squiggles and scribbles. You see such symbols embroidered on Freemasons' aprons in "exclusive" photos that accompany exposés "penned" six times a year by my esteemed colleagues.

Let me tell you, mate, I want to find him *really* bad, just to look at his unmarked nose and cheeks and appreciate, once again, my employer's ability to lie for no particular reason! In fact, this is the first thing I've wanted for about five years—but not enough to make its way into my dreams, mind you. I'm not a sentimental fellow by any stretch. Emotion isn't something I feel compelled to quantify, but I feel driven, what the self-helpers call *motivated*.

I've come to a decision. This'll be my last piece of journalism

5

before I kill myself. I haven't told anyone. Just you. So keep it under your hat, right? There's no one else to tell, I suppose. Every press rat in the country is on the Bryan Fix story. It'll be my swansong—not exactly a Walter Cronkite moment, but I'm a fucking tabloid journalist, you know?

They could've stuck me with someone less insufferable to work with, though: Cheryl, the twenty-one-year-old graduate with an eating disorder, zero work ethic and a shite attitude towards her profession. I'm sure she'll make a fine tabloid reporter.

Once the relentless spray of explosive diarrhoea is done, I pinch off one final column of would-be faeces before wiping my arse with the standard two-star Hackney hotel toilet paper—you know the kind, the sort that lacerates the anus with intricate paper cuts—and let the stench fill up our hotel room just to annoy Cheryl. As it happens, she barely even registers, just flares her nostrils and squints a little. Moaning-faced little bint.

"Who you texting, love?"

"No one."

"Doesn't look like no one to me."

"I told you . . . "

"Yeah, yeah, no one. You know, most junior reporters would kill to work under my tutelage."

"Really? How's that?" She looks up from her phone briefly, stops button bashing.

"Well, I been a journalist for twenty-five years. Pretty experienced and wise, some might say."

Cheryl snorts, goes back to her phone.

"Oi, Cheryl. Come on, let's play nice?"

"Fuck off perv!"

"What? You're young enough to be my daughter."

"Doubt that'd stop you."

"Good point, but still . . . show some bleedin' respect. We got a job to do."

"You old reprobate, I got a first class degree from a top university, what you got? You should be taking orders off of me . . . "

"Why you ungrateful little . . . Don't think cos you're a skinny bird with a blog that I won't rattle my hand across yer jaw. You show some damn respect."

6

That ought to show her. The cheeky cow.

"Now, come on. We're heading down Spitalfields market, see if we can get me a new t-shirt on the cheap."

"Why the fuck am I going with you?"

"You're a woman ain't ye? You can pick out something trendy for me."

Cheryl groans and reluctantly slips the phone into the back pocket of her arseless jeans.

***

After I buy a salmon pink shirt from the market, we head down the high street. It's ramrod cold, as per usual. She makes some crack about the cheap real estate. It's not funny but at least she's talking to me with civility. Just a bit of the c-word, that's all I ask.

I suggest we go to one of the galleries as a joke, only Cheryl thinks I'm serious, and when I deliver the anti-climax (that we won't be visiting any galleries as long as there's the illusion of free will), she becomes freshly pissed off at me. Since I've ejected my breakfast into the hotel toilet, my belly gargles for more stuff to be put into it. Shoreditch is great for shite food. Maybe a Ruby Murray would fill a hole. Too heavy. Maybe just a sandwich.

"Fix's dad is a trustfundist, very wealthy. Had a few properties around this way," I tell her. The phone is back out but mention of Fix's name galvanises her interest.

"Plus, he's cute as fuck."

"Steady on Cheryl, girl."

"Well, he is."

"Be that as it may . . . "

"His arse looks great in skinny jeans too."

"Amazing! A wealthy dad, a quiff and a distinct lack of talent, and look where it gets you! A place on the telly, celebrity status and residence in the hearts of every young girl in the country. Tragic."

"You're just jealous cos your old arse looks like a bag of wet cement."

"Oi, I'll have you know that my arse was quite coveted back in the day!"

"Yeah? Which day might that be, then? Day of the Dead?"

"Listen Cheryl, I'm a humane man but I won't hesitate to kick your non-arse up and down this high street."

7

"Pah!" At least she cracks a fuckin' smile.

"Let's find a pub. I need a pint and some cheap lunch."

***

Shoreditch is always under renovation. We pass a line of studio flats along Old Street opposite some of the shittier multishare housing. Winter has arrived in London. We all live in a place that is dusky, night eternal. Condemned beneath the shadows of a permanent eclipse, I can't even remember what it looks like to see the sun blister the sidewalk in the East during summer. Not that anyone misses it, you understand.

"This is Fix's last known location. I got a hunch he's hiding out at an old girlfriends' flat for a while."

"That doesn't make any sense, Fulton."

"Eh? Why not?"

"Because what self-respecting girl who lives in the dodgy part of a posh neighbourhood is going to let her spoiled loverat ex-boyfriend stay at her house while he lies low from the media schmaltz?"

"Good point young Cheryl. That's using your loaf."

The girl look mighty pleased with herself and I immediately regret giving her any encouragement.

"First, as I may have mentioned previously, we must find a pub."

Cheryl, for once, agrees.

***

Speak of the devil (except he's too much of a twat to be Boss of Hell), can you guess who I glimpse while we look for a pub? Or, at least, I think I'm glimpsing him, slinking about in that dank alley, over there. The only thing that makes me positive it's *not* Bryan Flitting Fix (and therefore not worth pursuing) is a certain distortion of his famous reality TV face.

I'm not talking about the seven-pointed and -sided polygons razor-carved in his cheeks and forehead, nor the stars of David with the all-important point in the middle, nor the swastikas reversed and rectified (looking a deal less sinister than usual), nor the spirals with exactly three and a half twists, all dug deep into his insufferably familiar kisser. (I refuse to believe *The Prattler* actually printed some facts in this case. Further proof this is *not* Fix.) That sort of mutilation is to be expected in a member of the "drugs subculture."

No, it's the expression on that face that makes me doubt my eyes.

It's the blushing, sheepish look of embarrassment, which, of course, is the last thing you'd expect to see contorting the features of a reality TV star.

Faux-Fix is shambling along in a smallish crowd of other sad cases, all with identical mopey looks and the same perplexities scratched into their faces, necks and hands—and, presumably, other bits covered by their unkempt clothes.

I see males and females, various ethnicities and "sexual orientations," as they are called, all similarly disheveled and demoralized. They walk along not chatting each other up, but are apparently accustomed to their own society, perhaps living a kind of communal street life. And, even more incongruous on these islands, various social classes are represented, hanging around together, including a posh-looking old dame, a ringer for the female MP for Hackney North and Stoke Newington. Looking a bit like the colonial upstart Hillary Clinton, but about one twelve-thirty-thousandth as mighty, her clothes and hair are not in the best of shape, but it's her. Trust me, I know, for I happen to be one of her worthy constituents.

Oddest of all, under their shirts and blouses, I see dull flashes of the same long-sleeved underwear, white and gauzy, unisex-style, stitched with occult doodles, that greeted us in the hotel this morning, prior to breckies.

Unfortunately, my need for a pub supercedes my journalistic calling, so I don't abandon Cheryl on the cobbles and go running after these obvious hallucinations for an interview.

***

We find a pub called The Wifebeater. A Bangladeshi fellow is vaping under the frayed awning, blocking passage. He looks us both up and down suspiciously. The bracelets on his wrists jingle when he adjusts his stance to let us past.

"Yo blud, you got some Chaz?"

"Sorry pal, dunno what you're talkin' about." I look into his nailhead eyes.

"Shoulda guessed by your garms that you weren't holdin'. Your missus is a banger though, fu-real."

"Thanks?"

"Wanna go bun a zoot luv?"

9

"Fuckin' pervert," Cheryl says as she squeezes past the letch.

We head in for a pint and a cheese sandwich. I'm Hank Marvin. Standing at the bar I try to get the attention of the barmaid but she rubber ears me. Then . . .

"Well, well, well . . . if it isn't the greatest mind in London."

I turn around to meet the smug visage of Billy O'Donoughie, CID (which abbreviates the name of the cop agency he snoops around for). Bill is an old friend, fat as fuck and pale as Banquo's ghost. Just like me. But, unlike me, high-voiced and suspiciously beardless—something like those round-arsed missionaries. And he's six-feet-ten inches tall, the carny geek.

(Need we cast our eyes into the shadows and check to see if he has disproportionately small feet? That is supposed to help you speculate on the size of his shlong—but the latter appendage's very existence is doubtful in this case.)

Billy O'Donoughie, CID, portrays himself to be all tough but he does everything in his power to hide the fact that he's really a corn-fed Essex boy, a gigantic perhaps-not-so-borderline hermaphrodite, and has two awful ex-wives along with an Adderall dependency. In other words, a cracking good bloke! One of the best on the force. We've known each other for as long as I've been in journalism, that's over two decades.

"O'Donoughie, I didn't realise they still allowed convicted pederasts into the force."

Always one to josh about sex crimes, me. Part of my job.

"Very good, Fulton. You're a dab hand at coming up with 'facts' on the spot aren't you? You gonna print that last comment as gospel?"

"Don't tempt me."

"Since we're both off duty, how about a pint of Stout? You are off duty aren't you?"

I don't want him to know a thing about my story, so I tell him sure, I'm off duty.

"Who's the young person?"

I turn to introduce Cheryl.

"This is my niece Abigail. Come on Abigail."

Cheryl is too busy on her phone to realise there's any sort of game being played.

II

"Nice t-shirt, Fultie. You mug a poofter in Bethnal Green?"

"Nah, just trying to be all metrosexual, you know how it is."

"Metra-*what's*-you-all?"

He shifts about uncomfortably, squinching his pudding-soft botty-cheeks, each one bigger than the entirety of my junior reporter, who still is unaware their owner exists.

"I don't expect you to be clued up on modern terms, O'Donoughie. Your lot are all still living in the dark ages."

"If this really was the dark ages I know what I'd like to do to your wee niece over there. Splatter my genetic inheritance all over her habit."

Somehow, his voice lacks conviction. What is up with this—er—*man*—in the erotic department? I'm afraid that even the tabloid reporter in me has a difficult time mustering enough morbid curiosity to pursue the question. But it would be a cracking good story for the front page: first the Mormons, then our own coppers—this *un-manning* trend, this fad of getting in touch with your feminine vagina, of growing hips and tits and somehow permanently shedding your five o'clock shadow without going to a laser specialist—it's getting out of hand, on both sides of the Atlantic. The scientists warn that the Y chromosome is shrinking, shedding capacity to store information—because that's all it is, you know: a thumb drive.

"Fuck off, perv!" Cheryl scalds. "You couldn't muster enough 'genetic inheritance' to make a postage stamp stick to flypaper."

Good instincts, this intern of mine.

"Easy Cher . . . I mean, Abigail. Mr O'Donoughie is just being colourful. He's famous for it."

O'Donoughie orders two pints of Stout.

"What's Cinders having?" He gestures to Cheryl.

"A Coca Cola for the sprog. She's barely out of her teens."

"Sure you ain't balling her, Fulton? Feels like a missed opportunity."

"I can see why you'd think that. I know incest is common practice in the CID. We still have some standards in journalism."

"I'd beg to differ, pal." O'Donoughie's face is chiselled in determination.

The three cloudy pint glasses appear. There's less head on

12

Cheryl's bloody Coca Cola but I start on the pint anyway. O'Donoughie and I quietly sip from the froth around our Stouts. It tastes flat, the barrel has been left too long. When the froth is gone I taste big chunks of yeast and protein. Fucking putrid.

"This pint is bollocks."

"The manager in this place collects all the drips from the real ale, the bitter, guest bitter and the mild, and pours it into the mild barrel at the end of the night. This is only four percent stout."

O'Donoughie, suddenly an encyclopedia of essential information, gestures toward the back of the bar, to get me to look away from my glass long enough for him to slip some of that same blue powder the missionaries tried to fob off on me back in the hotel. Why am I not surprised?

Cheryl cocks a keen eye at me, for she's seen the attempted doping, too. I quietly shove the pint away. First time in history anyone has seen a *Prattler* employee do that. O'Donoughie decides to play it coy.

"Classy joint," he says.

"This place is full of art tourists."

"Heard you got yourself embroiled in a nasty defamation case."

I knew he'd bring that up.

"They felt I violated the basic routine journalistic practices. A deposition was sought by attorneys, it was all very bloody embarrassing."

"I can imagine. Respected cunt like you.

"Yes, well . . . how're the hardy O'Donoughie boys, apples of your cocked eyes?"

O'Donoughie has two adopted kids. Apparently he was never able to have any himself. Poor, sad, obviously bollocksless morfadyke. I've seen both his lads—textbook-perfect specimens (if you like that sort of thing): blond-hair, blue-eyes. They could be illlustrations in a propaganda pamphlet approved by Joseph Goebbels himself.

Our policeman must enjoy good grease with one of those so-called "children's service societies." Or maybe he's just exerting clout, the cop's prerogative. He's holding off busting them for the white slavery enterprises everyone knows they're fronting for. Shaking them down for two free samples of prime merchandise.

Most adoptive parents would prefer to rent out a proper infant, before the little monster can be permanently screwed up in the orphanage. But if Mummy and Daddy insist on a newborn, they wind up—let's speak frankly—with the somewhat less popular colorations, sub-Saharan and so forth. If Mummy and Daddy hold out for a northern European profile, they have to settle for mordadykes with spina bifida, or else teenagers, tattooed and pierced, writhing with those abbreviated brain problems that need pricey pills.

Not O'Donoughie, the proud dada of two members of the vanishing, out-bred Aryan Ideal. I'm trying not to rise up and kick him where his nuts should be, the racist git.

He's blabbling about his unisexually-named rent-a-spawn—

"Jocelyn's working as a tech start-up in Glasgow. He does software, designs, sales, business, development, a little bit of everything. Evelyn works in a jet lab by day and a radio station at night time, and—"

I shake myself out of the catatonic stupor that such family-oriented chit-chat always sends me into, long enough to say, noncommittally—

"At least they avoided the Beat."

"Speaking of the job, you hear about this guy Fix?"

"Never heard of him," I lie.

"Thought your lot would've been all over this like a rash. Anyway, this reject is on the UK's number one mongoloid narcotizing telly hour and he only amscrays the night before the final nominations."

"Is that the Crack Den thing? I avoid reality TV."

This is actually true, although I don't know why I look down on that sort of thing. Seems right up my alleyway, and I'm hardly one for principles and high art.

"Anyway, this morning I get a call to come down to Pink Martini's, you know that club in Hoxton Square?"

"I think I know the one . . . "

"Well, we found a body in the toilet of the club! The corpse was castrated, cut to ribbons, had all these religious looking symbols scratched into his flesh."

"Jesus . . . "

"Yup, you guessed it, Bryan bloody Fix."

This seems a little odd, considering who I just maybe glimpsed moping about in the alley. I'll believe the booze-bleary corner of my eye before the cops' crime scene investigators any day. And, as for DNA "proof of identity"—well, you can just toddle off to America and ask for spit samples from the nervous ethnic Africans who overcrowd death row. You'll find one murderer out of a thousand. Sounds like the coppers "guessed it," too—incorrectly.

But, the skin excavation . . . that seems to be going around.

"Did your boys get pix?"

Seems like a bit of a statement to me, but I'm no copper. I'm dying to see some of the images from the crime scene in that Pink Martini bathroom, but I know O'Donoughie will never share any of the snaps. We have a weird professional respect but it doesn't extend to sharing information. We're both too ambitious to trade notes.

Imagine though, what a great story it would be if we had an image or something connecting Fix's (or pseudo-Fix's) death to some ritualistic sacrifice. That would be one hell of a farewell story.

My swansong just got interesting. Maybe. Perhaps.

**

Cheryl and I cross back into the fancy part of town. No one likes Shoreditch. People only come here as some sort of ironic exercise in nostalgia slumming. I hate it the most, though. I hate the upcycled furniture, the microbreweries and the shite seventies suburban art. I hate the creative class, those flannel-clad Hipsterpeneurs who turn everything into indistinguishable garbage. If Notting Hill is the "Bankers' Ghetto," then Shoreditch is the "Wankers' Ghetto." Croydon and Peckham will be next, you heard it here first.

In my disenchantment I bring out a stubby pack of Blues and pass Cheryl a lit cylinder. We both smoke in contemplative silence for a few minutes. I burn a hole in a receipt and it shrinks into a paper ball before disintegrating completely into a puff of sapphire vapour.

"Your boy Fix is supposed to be dead, Cheryl. Someone is reputed to have gotten to him and cut him up like a Christmas ham. Lobbed his ding-dong off. Or maybe lobbed off a ding-dong belonging to someone who does not wander about alleyways with female MPs for Hackney North and Stoke Newington, but looks a lot like Fix, after being used as a scribble pad by a crazed Freemason."

"Meh." She shrugs and takes a draw from her fag. The girl has potential.

We happen to stumble reluctantly past the flashy, pointy, stainless-steel campus of London Metropolitan University, where degrees are handed out stapled to mini-packets of nose-wipe, so people will take them. The sound of annoying protesters can be heard outside what academics these days refer to as an "open house"—a rag-tag gathering of youngsters who'd rather be in Oxbridge. In this case, for reasons a self-educated man of the world like me cannot fathom, the kids are in fancy dress, Haloween-style costumes. The fashionista in Cheryl finds it amusing.

"What's all this racket about?" she asks, as she nips the last of the burning filter and flicks it to the curb.

"Fuck knows. See that guy? He's a pain in the arse."

I point to Joe Nicoleaky, who I recognised straight away. Joe is an easy guy to like, as long as you're on board with whatever issue he's rallying behind at the moment. He's also head of the Afro-British Cultural Centre here at LMU (speaking of DNA and "identity"). Some people think he is a hyperactive dilettante, or, at best, an annoying Social Justice Warrior. I agree with "some people." There's something insidious about him. No one is *this* good without an agenda.

A girl dressed as a geisha goes flush red with embarrassment at Nicoleaky's reverse-racist rant. A colonial Pilgrim shuffles away from the crowd. Is that what Joe wants? Aren't we adults capable of making our own decisions without this arsehole telling us what to wear to our own Halloween party? Now, I'm all for gay marriage and racial equality, but this guy gets right on my Thrupenny Bits. If ever there is social injustice, Nicoleaky will be there. He stands out a mile in among all those students. He's forty-five forchristsakes!

He's waving a red and white placard that screams—

DON'T LOOK AWAY!
DITCH THE SEAL!
DITCH IT NOW!

Why don't blokes like Nicoleaky get accosted by whoever followed "Fix" into his last visit to the loo? Maybe next week. Never too late.

He thrusts his sign high into the air, his clipped Estuary accent rumbling above the chanting choir of students and faculty deans like a bowed contrabass. Angry shadows cascade against the open house. I must admit, Nicoleaky is like a fucking man possessed. Even Cheryl takes notice.

"Oh, look," she yawns, "big boy has another poster to wave in our faces instead of his dick."

ISAAC WAS A RACIST!
DITCH THE SEAL!

I ask one of the women standing around the open house what all the commotion is about. She tells me Joe is rallying with his fellow brats in protest of the college emblem, which includes the family crest of Isaac Swarthy III, nineteenth-century slave holder who endowed the school's first professorship. Following the abolition of slavery in British colonies in 1833, Swarthy III received the biggest single compensation payment issued to a slaver—a significant sum, most of which he pumped into the borough's local education system, including the university these students currently attend.

I guess hypocrisy is the compliment vice pays to virtue.

The protesters, unnaturally muscular cunts, all heaped deltoids and bulging quads through tight cargo pants, gather in the courtyard outside the open house, in an effort to attract new supporters from the crowd of prospective students. We watch two new freshmen recruits, athletic and lean themselves, pick up a placard each before joining in the chant.

At least the testosterone crisis has not reached all levels of society. The besieged Y chromosome has found its last refuge here in lower-middle academe. Cheryl seems especially pleased to notice this.

"A nine-incher, at least, that one," she coos like a tweeny from Chelsea.

"More protesters. It's like the sixties never happened." I feel myself almost snarl when I say the S-word. "This isn't a bloody centre for Marxist indoctrination, Cheryl love. We should really go say something. Get their fucking scholarships revoked or . . . "

"You crotchety old Tory grampa. Either listen to them or the best you'll get is sensitivity training."

She's right again. Surprising the number of sleazy pseudo-journalists are reactionary crypto-fascists at heart. I am no exception. I want to yell over at Joe Nicoleaky and his band of miserable Bolsheviks, but hold my tongue. I should be setting an example for young Cheryl. I turn my nose up at his Patchouli aroma.

He paints himself as this blue-collar troubadour, rough around the edges but hard-working, and—for that reason only—athletically built. (No gym time for Joey.) He's up to something. I know I'll see him in Hell. Preferably with his face all hieroglyphed up like a Most Worshipful Grand Master's lap doily, and his no-dout outsized junk deposited elsewhere.

"Remember last month, the hunger strike? The March of Resilience? It's people like him who incite riots, Cheryl."

"Mustn't let the lumpenproles express themselves," she sneers. College girl.

I don't care half as much as it sounds. I'm really just making my intern aware of this slippery hustler, as a type, in transit, so to speak. Part of her on-the-job training. We'll likely not re-bump up against Nicoleaky any time soon—not in this incarnation, at any rate.

***

Me and my slightly pinko sidekick and I are preparing to head out undercover. *The Prattler* sent us some disguises. We're going fancy-dress, like the LMU dupes.

I got a plain white polo shirt from Burtons and semi-expensive pair of G-Stars to wear, to make me look a bit more young and hip. In this getup I'll infiltrate Pink Martini's, scene of the alleged crime allegedly perpetrated against the alleged Bryan Fix.

Cheryl's costume, which I don't want to look at, will help her do her similarly sneaky job. She's to infiltrate a women's dildo-shop-cum-fuckbook store in soon-to-be-formerly-hip Hoxton Square. The place bears the neither tasteful nor excessively clever name of Comparative Lit / Imperative Clit. Cheryl will get us an interview with one of the reputedly divine misandrists who run the place like a lascivious and no doubt dykey convent. "Ipsissimettes" is how they identify themselves collectively, a word that has so far found no place in *The Prattler*'s style sheet, my de facto bible. I'm willing to assume it refers to some sort of urinary behavior that transpires in the back room.

20

Why am I sending the poor child to such a den of iniquity? Well, at the scene of Fix's reputed fucking-off from Earth, O'Donoughie's keen-eyed forensic pathologist noticed an anatomically correct strap-on phallus, varicose veins, gaping pores and all, lodged in the reality TV star's eye socket, skull-fuck-wise. (Left eye socket, not right, which indicates black magic. White magi fuck the right side, as everyone who's not an irreligious twat knows.) There's only one place in Hoxton Square that provides such equipment.

Furthermore, a fake fingernail was broken off in the harness buckle. This indicates, to the sexist eyes of us, the penis-encumbered, that a mechanically-challenged female might be the perp. This bit of plastic vanity was, according to the police report, painted a lurid amethyst hue peculiar to the cosmetic counter of Comparative Lit / Imperative Clit: a house blend, with which Cheryl is familiar, being the tasteless narcissist that she is.

Eventually I convinced her to scrape all that foundation and blusher off her sullen little dish, and to pose as a stringer for the infamous artist-run, non-profit, consensus-governed feminist zine *Bush Review*. She wasn't happy that I got to stake out the nightclub while she had to "make like a stodgy, unshaved slag with cobwebs growing across the entrance to her uterus." (Those are her words, not mine. I am not a sexist, once you get to know me.)

Cheryl couldn't be trusted to remain professional with all the tight-jeaned affluent young totty on show at Pink Martini's. Otherwise, I actually would be pleased to trade assignments with her. I could check in with my pleasant acquaintances at the sex emporium. I wonder if Susanna the cashier, the self-styled "High Priestess of the Ipsissimettes," remembers me.

Yes, I confess. I have penetrated Comparative Lit / Imperative Clit many times, like a brick and mortar womb, to check out what the stiffs at London Metropolitan University call "consumer items," and the Oxbridgers call "artefacts." All that stuff is in the front of the shop, where the exoteric vulgarians like me are permitted to go.

Rumor maintains that, in the back room of "The Clit" (as the place is affectionately abbreviated by every perv in the borough), are the sublime arcana, the magickal paraphernalia. Since I am so intimate with the stuff out front, I am hoping my girl can sneak in back and find us the sort of fine-edged gear required for blood eucharists .

***

Pink Martini's considers itself a relatively high-class joint. You have to go down a glass staircase to the basement of Morton's Private Members Club. Martini's has about five thousand square feet of flamboyant design, spread over two floors, and has a founding committee that reads like a who's who of London's bratty aristocracy. It's been ornately refurbished to resemble (significantly?) a Masonic temple, and even I balk at its hideous grandeur. I hear a guy in the queue at the bar describe it as "formidable." I suppress my gag reflex as expertly as Linda Lovelace, and start up a conversation with him.

"Hi old bean. Did you hear about the ghastly murder business last night?"

"I'm sorry?" he says, literally looking down his long snout at me. I continue talking to the underside of his chin.

"It's just, I heard there might be the threat of foul play."

"I'm sure I don't know *what* you're talking about." The toff turns his back to me. I put a hand on his shoulder and squeeze.

"Come on mate, let's play nice."

"Are you a policeman?"

"No. I'm twice as contemptible as that lot."

"You're referring, are you not, to that so-called actor on the telly? The fellow, what's his name?"

"Bryan Fix . . . "

"Yes. They cordoned off the gents. Heard he'd been slashed or something."

"Were you in here last night?"

"Just briefly. My friend Michael might know. I say, Michael—"

An aged hippie approaches the bar. I know this cunt too. Michael Redford, total drug fiend. He's under the impression he exudes righteous knowledge, possibly because his grandfather was once in-house chemist for the Grateful Dead many moons ago—or so he'll tell you if he gets half a chance. When I knew about him, he had this five hour energy routine and microdosed psychedelics before going to work. A real radio rental.

He'd take 0.5g of mushrooms to reach a subperpetual level of ecstasy, just enough to keep him from seriously tripping. He always considered himself a self-reporting experimenter. Redford was a pharmacist by trade, dealer by economic necessity.

"Well, well, well . . . Michael Redford," I say, as if we're old muckers.

"Have we met?"

"I'd say we have! You're none other than the Quack of Dover! Famously arrested for selling hydrocodone, oxycodone and ketamine for a profit about five years ago. Coppers charged you with drug trafficking, possession of drugs with the intent to sell and, of course, selling, you clever dick, you."

"I don't do any of that anymore. I make an honest wage."

"Hey, I'm not here to judge you, pal."

"Good, because I've paid my dues."

"Of course, with tip included. Meanwhile, your boon companion here seems to think you might know what went down in the Khazi last night?"

"In the what?"

"The toilet. That bloke who got murdered. Did you see anything?"

"No, of course not. One minute I'm picking up a cran-apple spritzer, the next a swarm of policemen are ushering everyone out of the club."

"I see."

"So, I didn't see anything that would be useful to you Mr . . . ?"

"Fulton."

"And you're a . . . ?

"Sagittarius. Now let's cut the bollocks. You were the biggest dealer in West London, sold to all the big celebs. You sure you didn't know Mr Fix?"

"Of course I'm sure. My most regular clients were churchgoers."

"Looking for a little help in achieving the spiritual experience, eh?"

"Oh, these weren't Christians."

"No?"

"No. They were part of some Hackney cult. I really don't know any more about it. Something to do with blood and so forth. Unpleasant."

"You still got any phone numbers of ex-clients?"

"No, I'm afraid my caravan was burned down, my lab too, and the police seized everything else."

"Well, if you hear anything . . . be sure to notify *The Prattler*. Ask for Fulton."

"Of course."

Redford sidles off, perspiring visibly. I let him get ten feet away before I say the requisite, "Oh, one more thing."

He twitches.

"What's the word on a new medicine in town? Sky-blue powder being slipped in regular blokes' cocktails and pints by sort of eunuchy-looking types?"

Redford blatantly retreats, not even subtle about fucking off.

I order myself a drink, hoping to catch one of these toffs trying to dose it with the abovementioned "medicine," and meanwhile start people-watching. Someone must've seen what went down last night. There must be some connection. The symbols carved in the kissers . . . looked sort of like . . .

Just as the image of long underwear pops into my head, my phone buzzes into life. It's Cheryl.

"Talk to me."

"I'm in the Cliterarium Pit or whatever the fuck it's supposed to be called."

"And?"

"It's full of pervs.

"No, really? You're just putting me on, right? Testing my gullibility."

"I'm on the shop floor. Loads of advanced technical vibrators and ass-plugs, kidney dislodgers, plus weird porn videos and fucky books for sale."

"Oh, really? I've never been there myself, of course."

"You probably camp out on the front stoop. Anyway, I think you should get down here."

"I'll be there soon, love. Pink Martini's is a bust. No one's chirping. See you in ten."

***

On the way I pass the alley where I might have seen, or hallucinated, Fix, or his ghost, shambling around with his motley yet uniform crew, looking apologetic for existing. This time Fix's posture has improved, and his color, as well as that of his mates, including the female MP for Hackney North and Stoke Newington. They all look downright smug—I mean, the opposite of their previous hangdoggedness.

They look like those people in self-actualization pamphlets who have passed through what is called "the dark night of the soul" and come out the other end feeling fine about themselves. I liked them better before.

No, not smug. As Fix moves into a wash of sputtering neon, I see *beatitude* on his kisser. That is the only word. Like what you see on the kissers of saints in paintings done in the old days when that religious sort of thing was the biggest game in town, and beatitude was taken seriously enough to be depicted by the most clever artists. Fix and his crew are floating on invisible clouds of holiness.

No longer disheveled, they look quite presentable. Even their uniform long-johns glow more brightly through their outer clothing. And, under those better-kempt threads, their secondary sexual characteristics—beards and biceps on the one hand, tits and asses on the other—seem to have melted into one another, mutually moved toward a happy, or at least complacent and numb, medium.

The esoteric symbols on their exposed epidermises have healed and resolved into proper liturgical tattoos.

Perhaps best to move on and write this off as an acid flashback, a contact-buzz from being breathed on by the former Quack of Dover.

***

Comparative Lit/Imperative Clit looks like a department store, but it's full of these desperate men. I see one guy out the corner of my eye, a right Billy-no-mates, wearing a tweed jacket with elbow patches and spectacles resting on the bridge of his big conk. He's rubbing his thighs and clutching a copy of LOVELUST/BARELY LEGAL—THE HEADMASTER'S REVENGE. One guy, another menacing presence, is perusing the double-edge dildos while stroking a child's severed pigtail and muttering "Soon Synthia, soon," in a deranged mantra. Two young studs in their twenties, wearing matching Stringer vests, are sword fighting their cocks in the mouth of a crusty old spastic pensioner in a wheelchair. You can tell the three men are all related somehow, as they share this shamed, lost expression that hangs beneath the eyes in concentric circles. The smell is ungodly. Now, I'm no hygiene freak but, Jesus-

H-Christ on a turd sandwich, it reeks of sweating balls and fermented jism in this joint.

. . . No, if you aim your mug toward the mysterious back room, it smells of *burning* jism. (A familiar odor to former Boy Scouts like me, who misspent their youths having circle jerks into campfires. But why should I feel the need to explain myself?)

Off the shelves jumbo butt-plugs (with and without flexed barbs) are flying in a retail frenzy, plus solar-powered nipple clamps, ball gags resembling inflated *fugu*, asphyxiation masks, ghost pepper-tipped catheters, labia minora extenders, tubes of slightly abrasive diesel-scented lubricant and scumbags whose latex reservoir tips are molded into amazingly perfect likenesses of Idris Elba, quite racist—or "racialist," as our style sheet back at *The Prattler* insists. I think the document needs about a hundred years worth of updating.

This place is like a holding pen for London *Untermunchen*. I clock Cheryl's skinny arse talking to one of the staff members, and smiling. I never thought I'd see the day. The woman she's chatting up isn't particularly beautiful, nor is she the crew-cut tyrannosaurus you might expect. She's probably what you'd call a "yummy mummy." In fact, all the staff here look like youngish-to-early-middle-aged mothers keeping an eye on their kids while they mill around in a crèche. I wander over to get a better audio.

"If you're interested in joining the cause, we've printed a pamphlet that might sway you."

"Sure."

Good old fucking Cheryl. She's in. Credit where it's due, the girl's done good. I just hope she's not stepping into the matriarchy's lair. She'll be fine. She's a tough bird, if nothing else.

I approach the cashier, High Priestess Susanna, a frumpy woman with a kind plate face, wondering if she'll remember me from my sex-toy shopping junkets. She does not—or feigns not to. Still, I hit on her, figuring I should help my junior assistant get the lay of the land.

"Excuse me, I was wondering if you had anything with Laura Loveleyknockers in it?"

"Two minutes and I'll double check."

The broad's fingertips flutter along the keyboard of her computer.

"We *do* have FAT COCKS IN SKINNY CLUNJ in stock, have you seen that one?"

I *have* seen that one.

"No, I haven't seen that one. But it sounds *great*."

"I'll just go get it for you."

"Say, thanks very much darlin'."

"No problem at all! Laura Loveleyknockers is one of the best erotic film stars around. You're clearly a man of taste."

"Well, I always thought so. Try telling that to my ex-wife Sheila!"

"Aah, the unappreciated male. Don't worry, Laura will help restore some of that masculine energy and repair your fractured male ego."

"It's a fragile thing."

"It is."

"But not small."

"Goes without saying."

I notice Susanna is wearing a Spurs pendant.

"I see you're a Spurs fan?"

"You caught me."

"Hey, nobody's perfect, love."

Comparative Lit/Imperative Clit has a drink machine, and I am itching after coffee for my perpetual hangover, but no caffeine drinks are stocked, strangely enough. It's like visiting the unpronounceable American state of Yoo-Tah. Or is it Oo-Taw? *Puta*? I may be an ignorant twat, but even I know that means *whore* in the lingo that is fast supplanting the Queen's in that bastardized, adolescent excuse for a civilization.

No caffeine or tobacco. What is this, a Mormon harem? If so, they seem to have swallowed Brigham Young's voluptuary legislation. We tabloid journalists are distinguished by our thick-headed imaginations, and our inability to refrain from running with them, and then reporting our heavy-handed, lead-footed inventions as fact. Ergo, you are required from this point onward to assume that the staff of "The Clit" are all plural gay-married wives of Susanna the cashier. These are schismatic splinter Mormonette polygamist dykes. Chew that and swallow.

How do I know so much about this particular delusion among

so many? Why was I so well-prepared to face those two missionary intruders at the two-star flop house this morning?

I'll have you know that, your narrator, in his capacity as senior reporter for *The Prattler*, once infiltrated their branch temple in Newchapel (or claims to have infiltrated, which is the same thing in my particular genre of high journalistic art). That's right. I mugged a Mo-Mo in the loo of the South Kensington tube station and requisitioned his magickal long underwear, with intentions of a proper Sean Connery-as-007-style creepy-crawl, through air conditioning ducts and all that sort of gaff. But then, as usual, I got so drunk that I knew no better than simply to hop their ornamental thorn bushes and peek in the back door.

And the following immortal prose is the result. I hope you won't accuse me of excess authorial vanity if I quote a fair portion of my masterpiece at some length, as it has some pertinence to the present situation. If you are going to continue following me, your narrator, for the remainder of this yarn, it might behoove you to get a sense of his professional work. Besides, we are in a bookstore, which brings out the literatus in me.

So, here's a goodly slab of my masterpiece, as printed last year on the ever-so-high-tone pages of *The Prattler*—

***

Besides doing all those superstitious things that everybody knows about, like baptizing for the dead, such as Abraham Lincoln or Mohandas Karamchand Gandhi or Bertram Rustle, just to name but a few, they also have these wigged rites where they tie up these poor, sad minority-groupers that the SCO19 Specialist Firearms Command Vice-Army arrests for prostitution and being pimps in Marlybone High Street, Bryanston and Dorset Square. And they torture and maim and shackle and boil these poor members of under-represented minorities.

Everybody knows that the Latter-Day-Saints is very prejudiced. I mean like seriously prejudiced, like minority-groupers didn't used to could be priests, and they have to pay fifty-percent more tithings if they want to be members, and they can't step inside of a neighborhood ward unless they've had a vasectomy or a fallopian-tube tie off, as the case might be. This is because The Book of Mormon says Our Lord made members of suppressed minority groups "loathsome" because they are descended from Cain, who was the first wigged-out murderer in history when he did Abel with a shiv.

(I apologize for some of this slang. It's required by the fucking *Prattler*'s dated style sheet.)

These Mormons can prove who minority-groupers are descended from, because they have the family tree of every person in the Anglosphere traced clear back to Adam, and, what do you suppose? Hard as it might be to believe, every single solitary one of them M-groupers turn out to be the sons and daughters of this horrible cunt, Adam, Jr., a.k.a., Cain.

Whenever the Guv of the Church and his Council of Geezers come to town to see Big Ben (because they've got Big Bens on the brain, these polygamist satyrs), they drop by their franchise in West Park Road. To help their Heavenly Father get his Blood Atonement, they take these poor underprivileged dudes and chicks down in the basement of the Tabernacle, during Choir practice so nobody will hear the screams and howls, and they tie them up bare-naked on granite altars, and they have these huge feasts where the Members of the Council of the Twelve Apostles line up in their walking frames and wheelchairs and take turns ass-raping under-represented buttholes and smashing repressed heads with rocks and fucking discriminated-against brains, while the Lesser Quorum of the

Seventy sit around trying to make the ninety eight-year-old Church Guv pop a chubby. See, they have to do this, suck and tickle and give his dried-out balls twenty-minute hum-jobs, so he will be able to see God in the final climax-stages of the party.

They believe their Guv's the only twat in the world that can see God, because he's the Living Prophet, Seer and Revelator. Except he's all that good stuff only when his grey cock is stiff, which it almost never is, because he's so old. And somebody's got to really put on the elbow grease to make the cobwebby thing stand up, so he can talk to God through its pee-hole, and God can tell the Church Fathers how to conduct their business dealings.

(In this next bit, perhaps I overreached, delving into economics, which is not my strong suit, as you can tell by my polyester dacron suit. But, bear with me—)

Does our loyal readership know that the Church of Jesus Christ of Latter-Day Saints is one of the top twenty corporate entities in the entire history of worldwide fiduciary matters? That's right, it's a documented fact, and the Guv's prick is like a telephone receiver, a hot line to corporate headquarters, which are located in an attractive office in the Celestial Kingdom. And this hot line is activated not by a push-button, but by a big, drooly, backward-bending boner.

Except God says that lady Mormons, or 'Box-Elders,' as they're called by doomed heathens, aren't allowed inside the Temple to give the Guv such boners, because lady Mormons would get out of hand during the sacramental minority-grouper rites and spoil the sacred mood. Our esteemed readership is well aware know how cunts will get when us regular guys get them really hot and steamy, right? I mean, they just go overboard. Good taste goes right down the chunky brown streaked toilet bowl, right? Everything would just get too disgusting, and they can't have that in the sanctified Temple.

So the starch-Mormons are allowed to have just homo orgies, no gashes involved, on Temple Square, where they hack to tiny pieces the half-dead M-groupers and eat their livers and pancreases raw, mixed with Gelusil, a whole lot of Gelusil, because the old codgers' stomachs can't metabolize the Ten High and Thunder Chicken the minority dudes and chicks drank before they were captured and read their rights and baptized for the Big Holy Blood Atonement Sacrificial Hootenanny.

And they play Donny Osmond videos, except just the ones he made before he grew that little beard, plus his twin sister's pregnancy exercise videos, in place of real pussy. And it's like a fucked-up Eucharist, except, instead of chowing down on a dead Jew, they chew on live minorities. And this ceremonial observation is the only thing, the really wise old General Authorities say, that keeps Heavenly Father mellow and keeps him from sending an earthquake and killing us all in the Thames Basin, like tomorrow morning, because we're all such blasphemous sinners.

The real Mormon god is called Moloch, and, if you look in an unabridged dictionary, you'll find that the word Mormon is derived from the phrase Moronic Myrmidon of Moloch.

***

As you might imagine, I'm presently not on the best of terms with the local branch of the Church of Jesus Christ of Latter-Day Etcetera. This is why, earlier today, thoughts entered my head of sky-blue ricin in the teapot.

35

But, regardless of my profession as a dutiful tabloid hack, and in spite of my salmon pink teeshirt, my ass smelling like full English diarrhoea, my breath like cheap booze and cheaper curry, the staff of this presumably Mo-Mo emporium do not treat me with contempt. The only time I am treated less than cordially is when trying to light up a fag.

The Ipsissimettes must, indeed, be splinter-Mormons, just as I've been suspecting. Yeah, that's it. And when a reporter from *The Prattler* says "that's it," *that* is and remains *it*, as far as the great reading public are concerned, in their tens of millions.

As a result of the *chef-d'œuvre* you have just enjoyed reading, I was given my own personal hot-and-cold-running intern, or *schlep*, as Cheryl's ilk are called by our masters in the mass media. The musty little slit, benefactress of my Nobel Laureate-quality genius, with her "first class degree from a top university," thinks my article is "too heavy-handed, from a stylistic point of view." I need to beat that pretension out of her.

Speaking of beating (*off*, that is), this cashier, this High Priestess Susanna, is giving me a red hot erection, burning at the tip, like those good old nonspecific urethral chancres one used to contract three times a month in one's salad days. I haven't had one of these since I was twenty-five and fingering that barmy Fanny McLean against a skip behind a Tesco car park. That same anchor of arousal in my gut, that complete self-awareness. Yet this particular hard-on seems somehow more sociable than erotic: I've actually found a crowd that's not boring or pretentious. I've finally stumbled among women who don't baffle me. Susanna is about to run the DVD through the checkout when I halt her.

"Can I have a look at that? Just want to make sure it's got everything I'm into."

She hands back the DVD without suspicion.

"I'm sure it'll have everything."

"I'm into *faeces*."

Since this is a bookstore as well as orifice-spelunker boutique, I pronounce the f-word as if I'm spelling in the proper Oxbridge manner.

"Oh . . . well, it has that too. In fact, the final third of the movie is Laura Loveleyknockers taking a giant shite on a punter's chest.

36

But by all means, double check before you part with your cash. You seem like a shrewd customer."

"Cheers, love."

Cheryl has been in that back room for about fifteen minutes. I'm about to go in guns blazing when she appears with her middle-aged confidante. I turn away, pretend I don't know her. Eventually the Ipsissimette leaves and I can talk to my junior reporter.

"What did you see in there?"

"Shh, wait till we're outside, you idiot. We need to leave separately."

I duly purchase my copy of FAT COCKS IN SKINNY CLUNJ. No point leaving empty handed.

***

"Ok, we're far from the wanking crowd. Now what's the score? Are the Ipsissimettes fanatics or just delightful, relatable women delivering a service to the resident dodgy bastards?"

"Loads of sharp sacrificial knives."

Apparently my apt little apprentice had the initiative to take some furtive pictures of the paraphernalia and decor with the hand-held communications device that comes attached at birth to these "millennials," or whatever their generation is called. She assumes the objects and scribbles are religious in nature. But, as Mormonism is not a real religion, I have decided to call them faddish fetishes, or else extreme party equipment.

"Anything else of significance?"

"Mmm, not that I can remember."

"Really? You were through there for an awfully long time, Cheryl."

"Well they *were* transporting blood clots and half-crusted spunk back and forth. In these zip-lock plastic bags."

"Right . . . and, you didn't deem that information significant?"

"I dunno. I forgot."

"You forgot that you saw this she-cult walking around with bags full of unspeakable substances? Semi-liquid abominations? Cops put on Haz-Mat suits before they go near that sort of thing. You daft mare."

"Listen, I'm going through a lot of stuff just now. My ex, Trevor, is texting me again and my dog Foo-Foo is getting the runs every single night. I'm like, no way is *that* happening again."

"Alright, don't get your Alan Whickers in a bunch! I apologise. Now, if you would be so kind . . . "

"The woman I was chatting to was actually really nice. I think her name was Pamela or something. She said the splooge had been drained from worthless pigs like Bryan Fix."

"Okay, now that makes sense." I recollect the hangdog look he wore on first alley sighting. "Poor nut-milked lads."

"Not just lads. Pamela also talked of unworthy women. And unworthy morfadykes and unworthy individuals of all of races, creeds, colors and persuasions. It's a big operation. They are not prejudiced, Fulton, against your tiny weewee."

"Good for them."

Damn. No battle of the sexes here to beat like a dead horse. No routine of stock phrases to trot out. Gender inclusivity complicates the scribbling we must eventually do.

"And the pussy drippings are squeezed from female politicians and society matrons. Against their will, I'm guessing. But, who knows? There was a lot of talk about unworthy breeders. And then they sacrifice this yucky muck by burning it."

"Sidney Poitier would be appalled."

"Pointy-who? What are you talking about?"

"Nothing. Ignore me. Babbling Alzheimer's is a job requirement for senior reporters at *The Prattler*."

"Whatever. And the smoke goes up to their Mum Goddess. Like up in the sky, you know?"

"Where else? Nothing wrong with that! Can you get me up to Ipsissimette Heaven for a chat with this dowager deity?"

I'm assuming the little cow is having me on. But, come to mention it, that would be the journalist's dream interview. I mean, most men would kill to speak to Queen Quim of Them Wimmen, have the chance to ask her questions, to finally understand our bleeding Venusian companions.

"Anything else you've omitted?"

"Oh, yeah, it's coming back now—one of the walls was made of purple cloth, like a curtain drawn shut."

"Sure it was a wall, and not the absence of a wall?"

"And there was an altar—"

"Of course there was. Where else are they going to burn? In an ash tray?"

"—with a gas ring and a stove pipe, and another gas ring next door with a pot of Sanka brewing."

"Sanka? Shag me sideways. We're onto something here. Let's find a pub."

***

On the way I decide to have a gander at the pamphlet that the Ipsissimette urged on Cheryl, and let my head be baptized in a sectarian sea. It says, among other daft nonsense—

Sheila, the She-God, presides above the Hoxton smog, waiting for her light snack. Many are going to see the Big Wifey 'mongst many. Inspired by the followers of Carpocrates, the Cathars and Bogomils, the Chabad-Lubavitcher Hasidim, the Borborites and other so-called Spermo-Gnostic sects past and present, the She-God's special people hunt down, harvest and sacrifice—not humans, but human body fluids. Sperm and menstrual discharges are burnt and sent into the sky as offerings for Sheila.

And, drawn with great skill, full-color, spread across the staple in the middle of the pamphlet, is a titanic, fat middle-aged woman (the "She-God," I presume). She reclines on her blubbery but beautiful back, on a couch of air pollution over the very streets we are prowling at the moment. This deity is magnificently, magisterially dickless, like a knickerless Germaine Greer squatting over a grimy mirror, yet buoyant as a zeppelin.

The text provides some biographical background—

Before deification, Sheila was a native of Hackney, and an early convert to Mormonism. She became close student of Mormonism's founder, Joseph Smith, who was a bona-fide Enochian adept, complete with skry stone and amulet from The Book of the Angel Rezial.

She's dressed in the expected magic underwear, the long-legged

39

whole-body garment of white see-through cotton gauze. It's the very outfit I borrowed off the sod in the South Kensington tube station while researching my masterpiece of yesteryear, and the same as sported by the intruders into our hotel room this morning. Her boobs and other naughty bits are clearly visible through the thin, stretched-out material. There are holes for her Saturn-sized nipples to peek through, and magickal symbols are embroidered here and there in red and blue threads.

Sheila attained the status of a goddess by becoming one of the many wives of Joseph Smith's successor, Brigham Young, upon whose death, along with her sister wives, she was wafted into outer space to help the him populate the planet Kolob.

Her lower body is hovering directly over COMPARATIVE LIT / IMPERATIVE CLIT, where a wickedly drawn assortment of perverts is going in and out—including, I shudder to swear, *me*! She's grinning, or glaring down at us tiny silverfish, looking very appetized. Kind of a hot blush puffs up her full moon-sized face.

Having broken free of that planet's gravitation, Sheila has returned home to Hackney and established herself in the smog over Hoxton Square. She presides over the Church of Latter-Day Eugenics, whose members nourish her with burnt offerings of human sex fluids.

A double stream of thick, lurid smoke is rising from a chimney on top of The Clit, composed of two different streams that wind around each other, and mix and twist. One is red, the other yellowish-white. They rise up into the She-God's crotch, sucked in by her mammoth vagina muscles.

Below this masterpiece of western art is a further caption:

Sacrificial gonadular incense transcends into Her sacrosanct upper troposphere. But the She-

40

God won't deign to suck up in her macro-uterus if even a single puff swirls more than a handful of testosterone or estrogen molecules. Too much gender gives her endometriosis. The donor-victims must be, Darwinistically speaking, without worth . . .

***

Okay, I don't know if I should be worried about this, but the pamphlet makes perfect sense to me. A quiffed reality star/crack addict, such as Bryan Fix, who never thought a complete thought nor felt anything but watered-down emotions, has the sort of skimmed-milk running through his tubes that would serve this She-God's moderate appetites to a tee. Draining him in the toilet of a bar with the first name of Pink makes sense, not only "Darwinistically," but also because it's just down the street, no taxis or bicycles required to transport his thin beer, his pale yellow ale, in plastic bags to the back-room temple.

The only question is why, or *whether*, they continued the religious behavior to the point of "cutting him to ribbons," as O'Donoughie describes it.

As I say, women have always baffled me.

***

At the Wifebeater I order Cheryl and me a round of beer. We're both a bit cream-crackered so I doubt this'll be an all-nighter. Cheryl's done well. I owe the pearl a pint.

"Those girls weren't at all what I was expecting."

"You were expecting . . . "

"A harem of homely, ball-busting feminazi man-haters, murderous on account of their own sheer repulsiveness, both physical and moral."

"I'll have a pint of Fosters."

Good old Cheryl.

A beautiful thing appears beside me at the bar. She's young with dry, kinky hair; sloe-eyed, possibly Asian. She's wearing a Round Neck Long Sleeve Knit Top and tight jeans. When I look at her she smiles. My heart fibrillates.

I would say at this point that Cheryl fades into shadows, except I'm paying no attention to her. She could have flown off in a helicopter.

41

"You an art student, like Mick Jagger and those other rock cunts?" I ask lamely and anachronistically, although I think it's a fair enough assumption.

"No way. I really look that pretentious?"

"Well . . . "

Her accent is upmarket. Cambridge maybe?

"I'm nowhere near that pretentious."

"So what are you then?"

Tell me you're not the hallucination of an old man whose sexual allure, such as it was, dried up decades ago.

"English lit major is what I am."

"Oh, I am sorry to hear that. I wish you a speedy recovery."

"Specialising in Cowper's translations of the Greek epics."

"I'm familiar with his gland."

"But I do read contemporary stuff. In fact, I'm familiar with your Mormon Temple exposè. It has a Homeric quality to it. Poking Polyphemus' eye out in the cave."

"I've no idea what you're on about. But syrup is syrup, and Fulty's a flapjack."

We both have a giggle. She seems alright this one. Plus, she's pure, uncontaminated tutti frutti.

"You tried Blue Lotus yet?"

"Blue, eh? Goodness me, what might that be?"

(As if this non-drinker of poisoned tea and stout, and this reader of crackpot religious tracts, doesn't know. Luckily, I am too foolhardily fond of my new Asian best friend to worry about being slashed and wrung like a dishrag after I ingest this stuff at her sweet behest.)

"Nectar of the Lotophagi. Homer's drug of choice."

"Homer Simpson?"

"No, as in Homer . . . of The Odyssey fame."

"Right. Obviously."

"You like MDMA or ecstasy?"

"Sure, who doesn't?"

"This is better. Relaxed inhibitions, makes you chatty, sexier, hornier! It's not a psychedelic."

"You're having a giraffe?"

"Um, no. Homer described it like this. You ready? I've got it memorised."

"Oh, I'm ready."

I look into her almondy eyes and, I'll be honest, my guts fucking liquefy. The anchor of arousal sets in. This is the kind of girl who makes you want to live for eternity.

Once tasted, no desire felt he to come
with tidings back or seek his country more.

"My job's coming back with tidings. You a spokeswoman for this Homo's Oddity dope, or what?"

"No, just someone who likes getting out of her head once in a while. Got it from this guy called Redford."

"Ok, I'm sold. Where's the stash? Am I sticking this up my nose? Up my arse? It's not an injection is it? Cos I'm funny with needles."

"Steep this in your Stout. Here . . . "

The girl pulls out the expected satchel of this fabled substance and tears the powder into my pint glass.

As I wait for the stuff to stop fizzing, I say, with wisdom in my voice, "So, finally, you people (whoever you are—and I have an idea) have decided you might as well get straight to the point, eh? After several attempts to hoodwink me into ingesting this stuff against my will, all you had to do was ask. I'm game for any kinky drug. Except Viagra. Redundant, you know."

I raise it to my nostril, suck up some of the fume. Smells like lavender and camomile potpourri. I shrug, take a sip. The girl is penetrating me with her stare, turning from almond brown to beet red.

As I prepare to drift off and up, the last few twitches of useful consciousness in my brain and eyeballs notice someone at the far end of the bar. A familiar posh gash is slumming, strangely receiving a line of smooth talk, similar to what I've just been given, from a Ipsissimette-cutie interchangeable with mine, and seduced to sip an identical blue brew. I may have company on this trip—though I'd much prefer something a bit sleazier, more stinky, with some tattoos and piercings.

Yes, it's my elected representative sharing this bar, the female MP for Hackney North and Stoke Newington. She's reaching down between the thighs of her Hillary-esque designer pants suit (it's made of the same fabric as upper-end hoover bags), and removing an excessively drenched sanitary pad. I think our Member of

Parliament could stand to upgrade to a larger size of feminine hygiene product. No doubt suffering from what the medicos call "Body Dysmorphic Disorder," convinced that her nether parts are more petite and less capacious than they truly are. Her particular Ipsissimette-Blue Lotus pusher holds out a zip-lock plastic bag, for the rag to be deposited in, and sealed shut, for transport to—

"Drink up . . . dri—n——k———up———u—-u-uu———p . . . "

I start losing my balance. I descend from my stool. Eventually I lose my foothold on what some people call "reality." Cheryl, help me out, luv . . .

**

A Blue Egyptian goddess. I hear the pulsing of her labia. I see her silhouette. A dense vapour of red smog swirls around us both, fingers the air, forks and laps at the flesh, fills the surrounding atmosphere with transfused gender plasma. I feel something like grill bars beneath my feet, baking my heels like two big slabs of smoked sausage. Through the cloud of crimson I see her true form— at least what I presume to be. Her legs are spread like the Thames, revealing the violet petals of her full, budding vulva. I can't believe I'm standing before the Big Girl herself. I feel as though I could slip through the open wire grid at any time—but there she is.

"Hello," I utter in awe. "Permit me to introdu—"

"Empy-ton. Your name is Empty-ton."

"If you say so, ma'am."

Her voice emerges like a choir of military wives. Must be the Blue Lotus talking.

"Are you here to feed me, or to be fed to me?"

Quite a question, that. Enough to make the initial rush of the sky-colored herb sort of level out and bring me to cruising altitude. As this creature lies back awaiting her answer, I can feel me going from a more or less chaotic oscillation to what feels like my proper innate vibe.

It resembles one of those moments of extreme clarity, surpassing any induced by psychedelic or amphetamine, that sometimes come in the earliest stages of a catastrophic drunken binge, when you're lying flat on your back in the piss and puke at the foot of the stage in a live-music pub, staring straight up into the cosmos. The lead guitar's neck is protruding like a dick in a fist between your peepers

and the ceiling full of strobes and kinky-colored stage lights. The Pete Townsend-wannabe slams all his meager weight behind a power chord, which he lets resound for a few eternities. The strings wobble and writhe chaotically in a chaos of backlit, or toplit, squiggles, but gradually resolve, along with their sound, after the principal attack, to six perfect arrays of crests and troughs, textbook wave forms, as they achieve their resonant frequencies.

"I'll ask again. Are you here to feed or be fed?"

I use the old journalistic trick of feigning complete, instead of just partial, ignorance. "That depends on who—"

"I am She."

Just as that guitar chord, so does this She resolve. She, with an upper-case *Ess*, slowly morphing into the literal Blue Lotus, the vegetative form, the botanical aspect. Then She blossoms further, from petals to skin. The sultry, slim Egyptian lineaments of the blue goddess inflate beautifully to WWI zeppelin shapes (full-scale). Only once before this moment has your mere slob of a narrator-protagonist been considered worthy to see *She*'s true condition. The illustration in the pamphlet must have been drawn from life. The She-God is, indeed, a titanically fat middle aged naked lady, who happens to be long and broad as several dozen Titanics.

Her blue skin resolves to the white of a native Anglo Saxonette—made even whiter by the long-legged whole-body garment of raw see-through cotton gauze, precisely as per the pamphlet's illustration. Her boobs and other naughty bits are clearly visible through the stretched-out material. There are the holes for her nipples to peek through, and the magickal symbols are embroidered here and there in red and blue colored threads, gauged like ship's cables.

The woo-woo talk dissolves with her Blue Goddess guise, like Isis' veil lifting off the nude cosmos, like the curtain being drawn back from the Wizard in the Hollywood production that rounded up every midget in the world, recruited them as extras, and left them to sleep among the urinal mints at MGM's back lot. That's something like the way I feel, in comparison to my hostess: a pissy dwarf. Fortunately, *pissoirs* are my element, so I am not knocked off my journalistic stride. A true professional is this—*ton*, *Full* or *Empty*.

47

A more or less regular conversational tone develops under my skilful professional manipulation of our chit-chat, allowing for her true speech idiosyncrasies to emerge. (Invaluable intelligence for any interview: the repressed regional and class background of the subject is exposed by way of tongue, throat, teeth.)

She turns out to be (or to have been, rather) what sounds like a Victorian Cockney slum girl, the sort who pretend to faint and languish on the pages of Dickens when on the make and wanting to be mistaken for lower-genteel Pimlico pussy. (I may be sub-literate, but everybody's got a little Dick-in.) But she has learned to feign the same extreme occidental accent that came out of the missionaries at the hotel. Yes, the big girl is trying, and succeeding fairly well, to match those strange ways of speech that bring to mind the salt deserts and dead seas of Yoo-Tah, and the pairs of long john-wearing young men, scrubbed and crewcut, who ride up to your door on those one-speed bicycles and try to convert you to—what? (The blue dope's having a laugh with my short-term creamery.) Some kind of American delusion . . . Jehovah's Witnesses or something?

No, I recall: The Church of Jism Crust on Fatter Laid Taints. We have a large, airworthy Mormonette hovering here.

"My name," she thunders, "is—"

"Let me guess," I say, ever so chattily. "Sheila, right? Okay, so, hi there, Sheila. Know what? My ex-wife goes by that handle as well. Coincidence? Must be significant with all this religious stuff swirling about, right? Well, never mind that dodgy gash. I dumped her decades ago, and haven't regretted it a moment since. But you, on the other hand, are clearly a higher class of gash—er, I mean, person. Say, Sheila, you don't think I could ask you a few questions, do you? That Asian English major who drugged me (such a gorgeous bit of totty!) must've deemed me worthy of your time, to send me here. You guys obviously want to communicate with my tens of millions of loyal readers at *The Prattler*. And who can blame you?"

"Perhaps you willed your 'gorgeous bit of totty' into existence."

"I can barely will a hard-on into semi-nonexistence these days, old gal."

"But your *semen* remains thick. I can smell it."

"Is that . . . er . . . so? Thank you for the vote of confidence. As for my blood, well, it's no sublimed quintessence of the aether, either.

Years of boozing and clubbing with fatten up the veins and vesicles of us mere embodied creatures of a day. The full English breakfasts don't help any, either. So, come on, Sheila, our She-God in the Smog (got a Lennon ring to it!) . . . what's the score with The Clit?"

She nearly causes the Earth to shift off its already dodgy axis by separating her thighs in a conversational manner.

"No, no, dear. Not that cetaceous nubbin. I mean Comparative Lit/Imperative Clit. What's happening in their back room, as if I haven't already surmised?"

"Hmm. Off the record?"

"Course. Scout's honour!"

"Universal and timeless is the use of semen and menstrual fluids in magic, eaten, used as a lotion, or burnt sacrificially. Think of the Carpocratians, the Mohel Rabbis, the Manichaeans, the Vajrayana Buddhists, the ecclesiastical branch of Crowley's Ordo Templi Orientis."

"Do I have to think of them?"

"Certain pertinent substances are combusted to discourage reproduction amongst particularly worthless specimens, or magically to make it impossible. Instead of killing our victims, as other traditions have done since before humans evolved into humans, we just strip them, carve 'Mormon' (which is to say, stolen Freemasonic) symbols on them, and forcibly, or persuasively, deprive them of their sex sauces. The feeling is still of a sacrifice, but the donors are left catatonic with embarrassment, rather than dead."

"And loitering sheepishly in alleys?"

"Of course. And when they snap out of it, sometimes repressed memories of the experience haphazardly emerge."

"Is there a point, I mean beyond improving the Hoxton Square breed? Are you getting kicks from this, personally, or, rather, *godlily*, if that's a word?"

(I promise to check *The Prattler*'s style sheet, once I've nailed this interview.)

"I am beyond kicks. It has to do with levelling the playing field. It has to do with hunger. I need to be nourished by the combusted sperm and menses of uninteresting people without too much testosterone in their constitution, nor progesterone, nor the estradiol which is biosynthesized from the latter."

"*Gesundheit*," I say. That's the tabloid reporter's sheepishly charming reaction to a spew of polysyllables. In other words, the Archbishop of Canterbury will pass an IQ test with flying colors before I look that muck up.

The She-God squirms on her throne, suffocates an itch on her derriere. I notice that I am now kneeling, genuflecting and bowing at her feet. The pulsing blue vagina is a meter from me—or, at any rate, what my earthbound senses interpret as a meter. It could be a kilometer—for, I just realized, I am not on a grill or a hot plate in a dildo shop's back room, after all, but floating in the London sky. Hence my hostess' zeppelin-ike airworthiness, way up here over Hoxton Square.

I am engulfed up to the waist by the hometown smog that has been eating away at the twin nicotene sponges underneath my ribs ever since I was a wee lad with a face full of fag. I guess, under this belly-button-level of tainted air, my balls could still be swinging down there at The Clit.

"I see," she says, "your eyes roam curiously up and down my spiritual prophylaxis. Allow me to show you the most important element."

Flexible as a ballerina one-three-hundred-and-thirty-six-thousandth her size, she lifts one leg, unbent, vertically up, ninety degrees aslant her reclining spine, to show me a slash in the fabric, in the rear, over what would be her hamstrings, if she has any tendons under that entire ocean's worth of back-knee whale blubber. It seems to have been stained around the un-hemmed, fraying edges, with dried brown blood.

"Indicative," she announces, "of the scriptural passage proclaiming that—
EVERY KNEE SHALL BOW
AND EVERY TONGUE CONFESS!
Those words are bellowed across the firmament. (Somehow, I have to call it that, rather than *apple pie*.) Far below, a meteorologically freak waterspout, stirred up by this vast displacement of the *firmament*, drains the Thames, as if a nine-point richter temblor has sucked away a few hundred quadrillion gallons of the North Sea.

Out of nowhere, a Salisbury Plain-sized bedside table appears at her elbow. I look in vain for one of Cheryl's *Books of Morons* for her to read herself to sleep with, but I see, instead, a stack of books and magazines (not including *The Prattler,* I am relieved to report). From her gargantuan perspective, these publications are smaller than one-one hundredth of an LSD gel. But she has good eyes, this grand bird, and dainty fingers to turn submicroscopic pages.

The She-God's idea of porn is to look at pictures of, and read articles about, insipid, worthless men and women, bisexual-wise: politicians, pop stars, popes, pimps, etc., plus regular twats like, I suppose, *me*, whose diluted intercourse-juices will be easy to vag-huff and digest in combusted clouds.

"Do you ever fantasize about Americans?" I ask, trying to ease into the Latter-Day-Saint question. I'd be embarrassed to talk about such a delusion if it were my own.

"Trump and Obama, et al., go too far, like scat porn, making me gag and turning me off, unaroused and unappetized."

Rather than talk about the genre of illicit entertainment that involves the carressing and consumption of turds and diarrhoea, I adjust our interview's focus to every Englishman's favorite topic: manners of speech, and how they can peg a person unbudgeably to a particular social class until he dies of moral atrophy.

"Forgive my saying so, your, um, She-ness. But you seem to have taken on an accent like a movie about gay cowboys."

"Yes, you guessed right. No need to sneak around the issue. A hundred and sixty years ago, while still a mere mortal virgin (or, to speak honestly, as this is a yellow press interview, a *demi-vierge*), I allowed myself to be converted to the faith of Joseph Smith."

"Smart move. That's using the old foresight."

"Tell me about it. My excuse is that, at an impressionable age, I was unfortunate to be standing on that street corner, right down there, when a great woman was telling the passersby about a man with nineteen wives and more than one hundred children and grandchildren: the supreme spiritual ruler over ninety thousand people, who believed that he was in frequent intercourse with the gods—

" . . . *for the Mormons*," she said, "*are Polytheists as well as Polygamists, and their chief god is represented as living in a planet . . . And now, with Pilate, let us inquire, What is truth?*"

52

"This sounds like the days before pilots. Unless you're talking about steamships. Mississippi, eh?"

She sighs, releasing a gale that nearly topples the suggestively shaped St. Mary Axe, scraping the sky over there in the financial district. Several retail items in The Clit are modeled on that architectural brain spasm. I suspect She might sidle across and ride it, sybian-wise, from time to time.

"No navigable rivers wind anywhere near the parched place where we converts were taken. My Hackney born-and-bred sisters and I made up a disproportion of the Latter-Day Saints' early overseas converts."

"I understand completely, love. I reckon something about this town in those Jack-the-Ripper days made the few people who weren't too gin-pickled to move, want to be someplace else. Even if it was a New Gomorrah ten thousand miles away, writhing on the shores of another Dead Sea that makes the original look like Willy Wordsworth's Lake Country. But, er, how did you wind up like—"

I tried to make a gesture that was simultaneously polite, yet broad enough to span the visible heavens.

"Upon death, like all tithing Mormon males, Brigham became a god, with his own planet, and he coat-tailed his supernumerary spouses up there to populate the place."

"'Coat-tailed'? Precisely what are the mechanics of that?"

"When the time came, my sister wives and I were subjected to *suttee.*"

"That's not so bad. I squatted in a furnished bedsit with a settee once, and subjected several birds to it, and not one of them complained about comfiness, and—"

"Ignorant little low-count, low-motility man. Learn your colonial history. The rooster died, so his hens must be combustively dispatched after him—a familiar enough sacrament on the Hindu subcontinent, but more or less secret among the Utah Saints—"

"Oooh!" I shrieked like a poofter, "*that* suttee!"

Very unprofessional to show your cards like this. But, god damn! The pure-as-vanilla-cream Saints secretly do collective autos-da-fe on their sundry spouseys! Did you know that? I did not know that! Talk about adding pizazz to my swansong! I can see the headline now, bannered across the sky:

53

HOUSEWIFE HOLOCAUSTS IN MO-MO MECCA!

The sleaze journalist in my trousers squirts spunk at the divine revelation of this salacious detail. From somewhere under the layer of London smog that envelops me to the waist I hear Ipsissimette giggles and the crinkly-zippy sound of a Tesco bag. That means I must be—

Oh, well. Fuck that. It's worth it!

"Brigham, in spirit form, was posthumously inspired to found our Church of Latter Day Eugenics by his prehumous experiences with some of my truly inferior sister wives, and especially the half-hatched, subnormal blond-haired and blue-eyed morons with which they were populating our planet Bolok, which is Kolob rendered to arcane and esoteric code in a particularly unimaginative way."

"Bollock?"

"Of course you would hear it that way, you, whose ton is empty. Brigham dispatched me—actually, I was drawn by the impersonal force, the Action that rules the cosmos—to be reestablished in the air above the home of my ancestors, my place of origin, this particular square. I've come home to roost—

Oh, morning, at the brown brink eastward, springs—
Because the Holy Ghost over the bent
World broods with warm breast and with ah! bright wings.

"Don't worry your unfilled head about who wrote that. And I serve Greater God Brigham even now with his eugenics program. He still feels terrible that a little more control wasn't exerted over who got to have plural wives back in Salt Lake City. To this day gaydar has no function in our New Zion, our Lovely Deseret, where the Saints of God have met. That's how inbred everyone is. Lisping is endemic among those with snaggled jaws and soft palates. There wouldn't be enough matches in the world to light the sacrificial fires should we station someone like me over the original Temple Square."

"I've seen pix. Looks like Disneyland, all done up in cheap rocks. *The Prattler* does an exposè twice a year on polygamy—but we've never made up anything like this—what did you call it?"

"Suttee," she sighs.

"So, that's when you were, shall we say, launched, right?"

"Correct. And we rose as lurid red blood smoke, just as the existential juices of various people have risen from the chimney of our storefront mission center, down there, just under my pelvic girdle."

"But I've seen small mobs of your victims wandering about, undergoing creepy self-actualization, achieving looks of beatitude in the very same urban hellscapes where the pre-Mormon you slunk around in your tattered petticoats, time gone by and ago."

"Our 'victims' as you call them—they are more properly termed *postulants*—tend to be temporarily addled by the lingering effects of our blue eucharist, plus understandably embarrassed by dim memories of being involuntarily milked. They need a time incognito to get accustomed to being unsexed. So they patrol the Hoxton shadows for awhile until the full extent of their sterile blessedness dawns on them."

"Blessedness?" I search the recently emptied tubes of my own scrotum for sensations that might be so described. And, there they are!

"Oh, I get it, Sheila. Being rendered sterile in this overcrowded town—in this overcrowded fucking *world*, for that matter—is the same as waxing blessed and pure."

Too obvious, my epiphany, to require a response. Instead, she says, "All our postulants—male, female, both, neither, undecided, indeterminate, indifferent—are rendered susceptible to sex juice harvesting by dosages of Blue Lotus, administered in seductive circumstances similar to those you experienced at the hands of your 'gorgeous bit of totty.'"

"But why," I ask (already having divined the anwer to this question), "me?"

"You, Empty-ton, qualify for eugenic stifling by virtue of your full English diarrhoea and profession. But your booze-diluted spooge is not the only reason. We might need a propagandist in this new media age. And you, my son, are to be commended for service to Truth, in your unflinching research into my husband's faith. Brigham admires how you gazed so unblinkingly into the horrendous but necessary goings-on in our London franchise, and the resourcefulness you displayed breaking into one of his temples (almost nobody has pulled that off). But he asked me to tell you (he was smiling at the time, so no need to fall down and die of terror) that if you'd tried it in Deseret—"

"Desi-who?"

"—you'd've been beheaded on the spot."

"And fucked down the throat-hole. I know, I know."

"You've been Blue Lotused up here to me, in the presence of whom, like all your peers, you are having—or, rather have just had—your own idiosyncratic version of a wet dream. You naturally imagine this 'interview' as a career-making scoop, and have emptied your *vas deferens*, exactly as I intended, when something especially salacious and headline-worthy was revealed, by me, at the precisely correct moment. At the time period you groundlings call 'tomorrow,' I will be vag-huffing your low-millions of scrote-manikins."

"I feel so ravished, so small, so vulnerable," I hear a poofy voice squeal from somewhere in my throat. Not since the psychedelic sixties have I been so fucked up as to have no control over my own mouth noises.

But then a contradiction in Sheila's spiel snaps me out of poofiness and back to tough, no-nonsense journalist mode—

"Hold on a tic," I say. "What about the lady postulants? Do ladies have wet dreams that make them menstruate?"

(Now that I've heard the question, I feel like a 'tard schoolboy.)

"You'd be surprised," says Shiela, "what ladies have."

"Imagine I would."

"Actually, females being more, so to speak, *cerebral* than you lot, we just sweet-talk them into forking over a bit of their catamenia."

"Cata-*who*-ee-a?"

"Look it up in your tabloid's style sheet, along with the key words you are now about to hear, as I deliver the set speech of our faith. Listen, Empty-ton to the dual way our husband taught us to regard the Twin Materials:

```
Polluting, in the exoteric sense, and terrific
in  the  esoteric  sense—as  in  plumbing  the
terrible  and  terrifying  mystery  of  coating
spirits  in  skin,  that  miserable  necessity. Our
sacramental  vintage  is,  as  you  have  seen  and
experienced,  semen. Our  chrism  is  fornication's
```

less specifiable fluidic discharges. Our unleavened wafer is the monthly clot—also known, in Crowleyan magick, as the Elixir Rubeus, which is semi-correctly considered by the graduate school of Freemasonry to be the Whore of Babylon's effluvium. And, living, as you once did, in a town where some bobbies still patrolled their beat equestrian-style, you might now be able to divine the occult meaning behind the legend that Ghengis Khan, the future subsister on spavined mare's milk, parturated clutching a motherly scab.

"I'm no more a biologist than a lit-scholar, but it does occur to me to wonder how sloughed-off uterine lining qualifes as 'reproductive material.' Woudn't it be just the opposite?"

"It's traditional."

I must have looked skeptical or puzzled or amused, because she added—

"Symbolical. In the most ancient of times, pre-historical, when people didn't understand the nature of baby-making, they needed some kind of clearly recognizable, easily obtainable, conveniently transportable, roughly equivalent counterpart to *male seed*, but didn't want surgically to extirpate a whole meaty slab of uterus to represent the soil matrix. It's not a cannibal eucharist like the Christians came up with later."

I look back to see and hear giant sucking motions from her snatch muscles, as the female MP for Hackney North and Stoke Newington's fried tampax squeezings go billowing up into who knows where. Shades of *To Sir With Love.*

As a contemporary western industrialized man, I never knew full-figured girls could be so sensuous. Looking at her Mariana Trench of a twat, I see the planet-sized cervix I've been mistaking since childhood for a smog-reddened gibbous moon when stepping out of pubs at two a.m.

The sensation of burnt lady hormones visiting her by the tradesman's entrance seems to bring more or less fond memories of the hubby from whom she's been separated for more than a hundred years.

57

"Brother Young was a fine administrator and an admirable camp counsellor as we trekked across the Great Plains and the Rocky Mountains. But the man has no spiritual development at all, and perhaps even less moral imagination than our creep customers down there. Witness this heavy-handed eugenics mission itself, which he assigned me and my sister-ghost wives. Do you know how hard it is to ignite a sacrificial fire on planet with no oxygen?"

"Yes, but how was he in the ol' fart sack? Assuming the ol' fart sack was invented in those days already."

"Wranglers and cow-punchers all the way from the Tex-Mex panhandle to the Oregon Trail were naming their frisky stallions 'Brig.' Hence the obscene numerousness of his spawn.

"My one regret is that I wasn't selected by his predecessor, the true Enochian prophet, who started all this in the first place. Brother Joseph Smith was a bona-fide magus, an esoteric adept full of the secret wisdom, whom Aleister Crowley, himself a frequenter of Hoxton Square down below (before it got so semi-fashionable), studied and admired.

"And, speaking of semi-fashionability, there is only one way that the male contribution to the gene pool of Hoxton Square will be spared dilution. I need their ring leader, the thin-blooded one."

"Who? What's his name?"

"Naked and Leaky is his name, Empty-ton."

"Never heard of him. Would *Nicoleaky* do in a pinch? Got a bit of a tin ear for monikers, ain't you, Granny?"

I do see what she's driving at, though. "Naked and Leaky," despite his public posturings and self-assertion, has no more moxie in his blood than Bryan Fix did. His rallying the muscular cunts with the "deltoids and bulging quads through tight cargo pants" (I love quoting my own *Prattler* articles, even the ones that never made it through the editorial filter, as "too political") is just a way to disguise the fact that his semi-precious bodily fluids are thin as Fix's. His black tickle-gizzard would release a good light snack to send up to this smog throne. (I think her digestion is dodgy.)

"So, Sheila, love, if I bring him, or at least, his tiny millions of manikins with the swimming tails and DNA-bulging nuclei, to you, in smokey form, I'll have saved mankind, or at least the segment of it that pisses about Hoxton Square, way down there—and, even more importantly, you will grant me a proper interview, on the record, no topic barred from discussion?"

"Yes Empy-ton. Drain his no-doubt overblown phallus, make an example of him—"

"Without making a poofer of myself. Quite a tall order."

"—slash the symbol of my vulva into his forehead. He will be yet another of a long line of sacrificial ewes and rams. This is not the Blue Lotus talking."

She can say that again. Not the bloody Blue Lotus, anymore. That started wearing off with the *estradiol*, or whatever the Christ she said.

"I should tell you that I don't think I can off anyone, dear. I've ruined careers, made up vile bullshit that eventually got people killed just to sell a few papers, but I don't think I'm cut out for the whole physical brutality of murder. You know what I mean?"

"Who said anything about murder?"

"Who? Bryan Fix said it. Loud and clear, with his corpse. Your Ipsissimettes filleted him pretty good, just like all the other guys."

"Didn't I just explain to you that it's not only 'guys' whose sex sauce is being sublimated to aether?"

"I meant 'guys' in the unisex sense of the term. All the young 'uns say it that way nowadays, and—"

But Sheila's not listening. Too busy chiding the processes of my brain.

"Conclusion-leaping is characteristic of the empty, Empty-ton. Does this smoke I'm presently vag-bibing smell of phalli or yoni? Or have you been drunk so long you don't recall the difference? I'm told this smoke is from the female MP for Hackney North and Stoke Newington. I've no idea if she's a Tory or a Whig, or whatever you call them now, but it makes no difference. I don't involve myself in non-eugenic politics—a lesson I learned from watching my husband turn into an asshole. Moral anemia is the only requirement for recruitment by our Ipsissimettes. And the only thing my girls did to Fix was drain his man-paste, publically humiliate him and carve the relevant symbols into his flesh. We did *not* kill him. Nor will you Nicoteenie."

I suppose I've been laboring under homicidal misassumptions due to misreading the pamphlet, enough to deny my own sense of

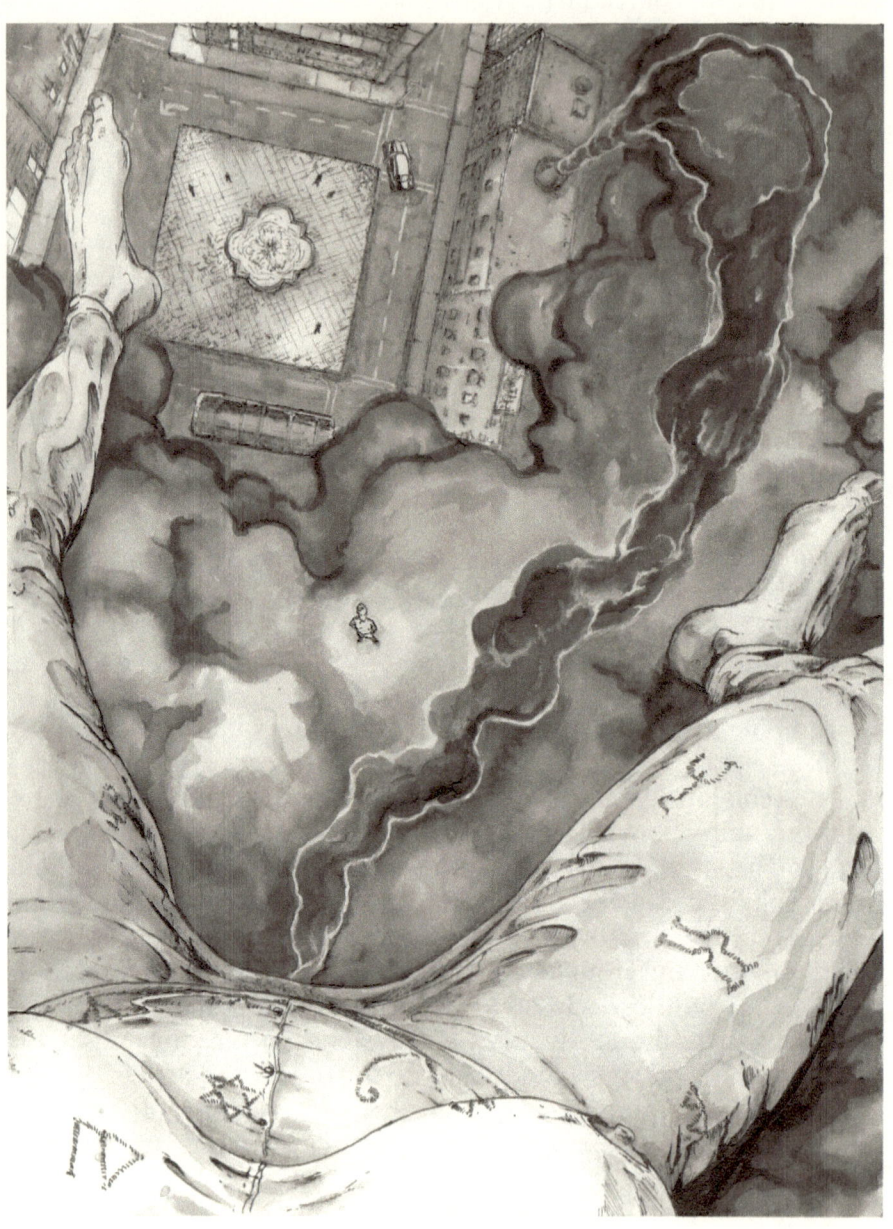

sight, which continues to pick the ex-reality wanker out occasionally, glimpsing him around alley corners, dismissing him—up till now—as a ghost.

"Then . . . who did do Fix?"

"Beats me. I'm not the bloody oracle."

The London slum girl comes out when idle *Prattler*-style accusations start to fly.

"Good to see you deities suffering from guilty consciences, too."

That miffs Big Bertha, and she suddenly breathes what sounds like a hex into my face, enunciating the X with bared, Cutty Sark-sized teeth—

"Hox-x-x-xtonnnn . . . "

The She-God looks into my orbits, shoving her eye-cock straight at my retinal man-vag, which squelches.

Apparently the Blue Lotus is starting to to wear off. At the hissing of our little London square's name, I feel the crests and troughs of my perfect vibe degenerate back to chaos. I plummet through the smog like an un-tailed spermatozoon, while, high in the receding sky, upper-case *She* resolves back to her blue Egyptianness.

And it's back to the daily grind of hangovers and full English etcetera, below.

***

Cheryl and I both got absolutely smashed last night. Hackney swings like a pendulum do (you-know-who on bicycles, two by two) when you've got some splinter-Mormon sacrament to devour. I must've been wandering around the streets in a drug-fucked daze, with any luck, not too shamefaced and apologetic. Cheryl apparently made it back to the hotel before me with her yardie ex-, Trevor—who subsequently hightailed it before I even came scrambling in with pre-full English gravy on the verge. Legs wider than Regents Canal, that Cheryl. Poor dear. I'm actually starting to like her, and listening to her add her post-fornicatory puke to my soup, as she's doing now. Living cheek-to-jowl with someone is good that way.

Common sense tells me that last night was a kinky dope-induced hallucination. Normally I'd chalk it up to dodgy gear; but that doesn't explain why I woke up caked in dry Aunt Jemimah batter and a satchel of Blue Lotus in my pocket, Joe Nicoleaky's friggin name misspelled on it. The little Asian student of Homie Erectus (or whatever the dead wog scribbler's name is), with her delightful mind-destroying confection, was trying to put me in contact with the Big Girl Upstairs, and seems to have succeeded.

The intermittent effects of being a newly initiated postulant of the Church of Latter-Day Eugenics come and go, like undulant fever. From time to time as I deal with my daily existence, I try not to hear my brain squeal, in a voice like Quentin Crisp, things like this:

The subject of my final article has become clear! I am intent on reporting, faithfully, The Church of Latter-Day Eugenics' plausible denials of taking part in Mr. Fix's execution. I want to help them. I want to save mankind. That would be a really noble way to go. Maybe the She-god will like my work, witness my devotion and appoint me Propaganda Minister when all this untidy unpleasantness is over!

Cheryl brings her head up from the bucket, foam bubbling around the edges of her mouth, tears forming and streaming down her cheeks. Absolutely Brahms and Liszt.

I swallow my inner Dame Quentin, force her down below my voicebox, and in a miserable impression of my macho pre-Sheila-interview self, say—

"Man-up girl. You'll be alright."

She belches at the rim of the toilet.

"Remember Nicked and Leak—I mean, *Nicoleaky*?"

Cheryl nods.

"Well, we have to pay him a little visit. Come on, grab some Paracetomol and get your coat."

I'm sincerely trying go get her up for the Nico leaking, as per my dream-mum's request. I throw her the rough pitch—but then, without knowing (but suspecting) why, and unable to stop myself, add, in a simpering lisp—

"That is, if you don't mi-i-i-i-ind, sweetie!"

She does what the Americans used to call a double take. Might have been a spit take if she'd had her now-usual pint between her tiny paws, or maybe a few spittles of barf left in her.

"Are you okay, Fulty? You're starting to come on like my grampa. When he got old like you, his voice got all whiny and squeaky and, sort of, like, all bend-over accomodating, and he started weeping at family restaurant adverts on the telly. This was after he couldn't hissy up a stiffy anymore."

"And I'm sure you were right there to be disappointed when that flaccid moment arrived."

That's more like it. The old Fulty is back. I'm fixing at least to threaten to kick her teeth in, but . . .

No. Empty-ton is simply too ashamed of his diluted self to assert it. Yes, embarrassed, in a sort of generalized way, is our Empty-ton.

***

The thing about being a journalist is that no one expects you to be all good and pure as virgin snow. I was a serial phone-hacker myself. I fabricated stories left right and center—I once photo-shopped a female celebrity's face onto pornographic stills which eventually went out as a front cover image for *The Prattler*. I've accepted dirty money to promote the administration's policies and willingly participated in cynical public relation stunts at the behest of crooked politicians. You should know that I often fake my sources, just sayin'. The ultimate unreliable narrator. I'm a bastard. Fuck, we're all bastards in this game, but we weren't all necessarily born into our bastard-dom.

I watched the most idealistic, well-intentioned get bastardized, just as the She-God watched her hubby Big 'n Hung become a bush-wah bureaucrat (though, I am trying to force thoughts of the Church of Latter-Day Eugenics away, so you can forget that simile).

I'll get to witness Cheryl become a bastardette, too—although I think she's at an advanced level already. The thing about our lassie is, she has a naivete that I think I'll miss about her when it's gone. Jesus, look at me, soppy as a lorry load of monkeys. I mean, sure she's a crass and unpleasant little cow who gets on my wick all the time, but she's also young and harmless. There's no genuine badness in the girl, and I can smell an overripe apple a mile away. I'll watch her evolve—the longer she's in this ugly biz—into something much worse than she is at the moment; something so selfish and shallow that her own reflection will make her stomach churn like a boat in choppy waters. Christ. She'll turn into me. If you let a media company self-regulate, you're basically giving it the green light to let it corrupt itself.

The She-God's postulant in me begins to sob and weep.

"Grampy started needing to wear nappies. Shall we stop by a chemist on the way to Nicoleaky's?"

"No, dear. Kind of you to be concerned. Musty slit."

"Mixed signals. He was giving those, too. The doc calls it 'emotional lability,' and it comes from declining prick hormones."

"Just keep talking. I'll try to make do with whore whines."

***

We head to the bizarre slice of stainless steel postmodernism normally frequented by Nicoleaky: London Metropolitan University. That's where the young and impressionable hang out, the lost virgin desperados who want to be part of something, and the heretics with daddy issues.

Cheryl and I arrive at the usual open house and I put out my feelers for a disruptive force. (I try not to notice that my feelers, like my nipples, have been feeling especially sensitive since I flitted down from the smoggy throne room.) Sure enough, he's there, chained to the railing outside the main entrance—the Great Goat of the Witches' Sabbath. Nicoleaky has bought a No. 1 haircut and is dressed in a T-shirt, tracksuit bottoms and trainers. It's raining two kinds of domesticated pets and Joe looks like a drowned kitchen rat. At least he's alone this time.

We approach him carefully, conceaing our bag of sacrificial apparatus from plain sight. (Picked our kit up from the back room of The Clit, where I seem to have carte blanche now—proud to report that Cheryl's observations were spot on). My cub-ette reportress must look terrifying in her hung-over state. In the absence of make-up she looks a bit like Myra Hindley, though she's too young to have heard of that rock starlet of the connective tissues.

Nicoleaky has a sign around his neck that says—

I'M ASHAMED OF MY WHITE PENIS.

And here I thought he'd been "self-identifying" (I think that's the term) as something a bit more sub-Saharan, in his capacity as head of the Afro-British Cultural Centre here at LMU. We've all got a squirt or two of high-octane melanin swirled in with our testosterone—some more than others. He looks terrible, as though

64

he's been chained up through the night. I try to make eye contact with him.

"My friend, are you ashamed too?" he asks me.

"You have simply no *idea*," I unwillingly reply in my Quentin Crisp voice. He and she both stare at me.

"Is your posture getting worse, sweet ol' Grampy Fulties?" asks Cheryl. "You never were a ramrod, but today you look like a ramen noodle."

Nicoleaky appears to concur. But he has his own emotional needs at the moment, and they need to be expressed—

"Then what's to be done? What's to be done when my penis reacts to children? How do I stop it from yearning after supple bottoms?"

"So, that's your self-criticism in this cultural revo-etcetera," says I. "Okay, I get it. Something drastic needs to soil your portfolio, if you're going to bring in the dupes when you come clean and see the light. Used to be mere adultery was sufficient. What's it going to be when baby raping pales? Something with cannibalism, I suspect. Or collecting and burning precious bodily fluids."

To my amazement, Cheryl brings a stiletto out of her purse and starts using the handle to bash old Joe's hand repeatedly until the thumb and pinky break. He growls at the pain, chokes on his own gargling saliva. Cheryl keeps bashing away, mumbling something about her ex-boyfriend Trevor as she goes. She tears his limp hand through the handcuff loop and, with all the adrenalin of misdirected love-rage, singlehandedly drags him down the alley that leads to University Road, me on her heels, trying not to whimper like Stanley being dragged into another fine mess by Ollie, role-reversal-wise.

No one tries to stop us. The locals must be pretty tired of this self-procalimed "gadfly," glad to see him go. There's one bloke sitting at a table outside a café on Mare Street, next to Hackney Town Hall, but he barely lifts his head up from his Frappuccino. A guy in a high-vis jacket with SECURITY on the back wanders past and pays us no mind. It's as though the She-God's got our back. You can see why, peckish as she always is. We're pretty much serving as her caterers at this point.

Cheryl brings out a wad of Tesco carrier bags—the kind whose distinctive sound I heard crinkling under the waist-high smog in the

65

She-God's budoir—and she wraps one over his head. Nicoleaky starts panting and the bag soon fills up with his condensed breath. Cheryl sticks her stiletto up against his ribs. Calls him "Trevor," and a "manipulative cunt," under her own condensing breath, rips open Nicked and Leaky's flannel shirt to expose his puffy chest.

The latter's crying like a little girl with a skint knee, begging her not to rip his Henley's shirt cos it cost him 125 quid from Lois Vuitton. Cheryl drags the heel of her stiletto across the ponce's hairless chest, carves out an inverted pentagram with martial precision, endowing him with the five wounds of Christ. His muffled screams seem pretty satisfying to my assistant cub reporter.

Then she wrestles his baggy corduroys to his ankles, licks her lips, puckers up, drops to her knees. What a consummate pro.

"This is for you, Trevor," she says before going to town on Nicoleaky's flaccid mollusk. He's not enjoying this at all. Think Cheryl might be a bit too old for him.

I decide to help the lad along with some verbal imagery I know he'll appreciate. Fortunately, my Fulty voice is back—for the moment.

"Come on you gutless wonder. Think about all those young, barely legal kids you chase after every day." (I'm just making this up; pretty sure he's never touched jailbait.) "Imagine all that tweenie totty fawning over you."

His prick responds, goes to half-mast and Cheryl works her mouth harder over the shaft. I have to smother a semi myself. Jesus, Fulton . . .

"No . . . please . . . "

Our victim's (rather, our *postulant's*) pleading tone kind of gets me, right here, just under the ribcage, between the nicotene hoover bags. Combined with my moment of self-castigation for getting a chubby, it makes me "waver in my determination," as the posh lady novelettists say. I avert my eyes, glance across the way, and see billows of *me*-smoke suddenly come sliding out of The Clit's chimney. Essence of Fulty is braiding in oily, yellowish-white ribbons up toward the big orange cervix in the sky, twining and twisting like a pole dancer in a fag bar.

My late shamefaced sheepishness and Quentin Crispiness, and my limp posture (even worse than normal for aging lush), are all washed away in a hot-cold interior (which is to say, *female*) orgasm of—what? Perfect *beatitude*, is the only word for it, worthy of Fix and his band of wandering alley gypsies on second sighting.

Cheryl, obtuse and self-centered as she is, cannot help but notice—the physical symptoms, at any rate.

"Have you been lurking 'round the tanning salons in Piccadilly?" she inquires around a gob full of no-doubt low-count, low-motility pre-jiz.

I start, again, to weep. With all the sympathy of a madonna on a papist trading card, I insinuate a reassuringly damp hand on my fellow postulant's forearm.

"I know, I know, Joseph, love. It's a bit of a hump to be gotten over right now. But, hang on, sweetie. Ride it out. Soon everything will be so—" I cannot speak momentarily because my entire respiratory tract is commandeered by a rush.

"—so *lo-o-o-vely, wonderful!*"

Cheryl is pissed. "Do you mind, Grandma?" She says to Joe, "Please kill me when I get post-menopausal."

Even Nicoleaky snaps out of his assault-victim mode, just long enough to give me a puzzled glimpse through the corer of one eye, as if to say, "What, in the *fuck*, is up with you?"

That snaps *me*, too, briefly out of it.

"This is so embarrasing!" I whimper.

With a sheer grunt of physical will, I faucet on what must be one of the absolute final squirts of manliness dwindling in my veins.

"Let's get this over with, shall we, girls?"

A minute passes and Nicoleaky declares that he's about to cum. Cheryl brings out a Sterelin specimen bottle and yanks on his plunger till a measure of ejaculate ebbs out and half-fills the container. His squealing finally abates as the tail-end of the orgasm shudders through his body. The Tesco bag rips over his head and he gasps in agonised pleasure as oxygen re-fills his lungs. Cheap rubbish those Tesco Value bags.

"Open your mouth."

"Eh?"

"I said open it!"

Nicoleaky reluctantly gaps his big political harangue-sputtering yapper.

"Please, I can't. I'm on hunger strike."

"Shut up, you tart."

I retrieve a thermal flask of Blue Lotus-spiked coffee and, ever so gently, attempt to persuade him to swig it.

Cheryl says, "Fuck you," snatches it from my oddly weak grasp, and pretty much hammers it all the way down to the sub-basement of his duodenum. She and I watch Joe's eyeballs widen to erupting planetoids as he climbs the Hoxton troposphere, on his way to visit my mum.

***

I guess we wait now. See if Sheila is happy with how we orchestrated her sacrificial quim-snack. And we know just where the waiting ought to be accomplished.

Cheryl and I have got used to the Wifebeater. Its faux-dank-charm and art student clientele are as much home to us now as the horrible B&B's *The Prattler* send us to. It's become our local pub. The Wifebeater, our legendary battlecruiser. Rub-a-dub.

I lay a crisp Lady Godiva flat across the counter and the barmaid collects it with her left hand, replaces it with a tall glass of frothy Stout with her right. Stoutness is what I need to keep my Fultiness to the fore. Not so much worried about my inner Quentin Crisp lisping to the surface as the beatitude that seems to have replaced it, which is even more embarrassing. A good basic level of drunkenness is the best defense. Nobody's lurking around with redundant packets of blue powder.

Speaking of Crispy Quenty, I see Bill O'Donoughie and go over to ask him how the Bryan Fix case is going. I suspect he and his cronies will be so off track that I'll have to struggle to contain a smile.

Sure enough—

"Utter shite. Virtually no leads. Not that I'd share them with the likes of you."

I grin and sup my Stout. Cheryl is at the jukebox assembling an eighties playlist with a nicker I gave her.

"What about you, Fulton? Any luck with this fucking Fix fiasco? I hear a group of fanatical teenyboppers have clustered outside his old studio apartment and are trying to use necromancy as a means of finding his location, can you believe that?"

69

"I'm pretty open minded about communing with dead cunts. Formerly dead ones, too."

"Can you imagine, though . . . being so popular that young women will consider using witchcraft to make sure you're safe? Must be amazing. Coasting through life like the blue bee on Krishna's forehead."

"You having a dry spell, mate?"

O'Donoughie looks all flushed, embarrassed. (How I *do* know the feeling!) In twenty years I haven't seen this git blush. Come to think of it, though, he's never mentioned his ex-wives. As a journalist you'd think I'd try and probe this subject. Maybe he's gay. Might explain a lot. Maybe the poor sod's in denial. Can't be easy being a queer copper.

"You know the Middle-English word for cunt?" I ask.

"It's on the tip of my tongue."

"*Queynte*. Like Queynetin Crisp. It's what you call a paradox. There should be a Cockney rhyme for that. How long have we known each other, O'Donoughie?"

"Too bloody long." He winks and raises his pint glass at me.

"So, listen. Can I ask about your ex-wives? Not a sore topic I hope? Figured you'd have brought it up at some point so we could rip into you for it."

"I dunno, Fulton. It just . . . never came up."

"Didn't put you off women did it? I've been heartbroke myself, believe it or not."

I feel postulant tears well up, but a faceload of stout washes them back. Not the right time for one's feminine side to emerge. This vast poofter could mount and crush me like a cigarette butt with lip gloss on the tip.

But, somehow, O'Donoughie seems to know what's up with me, what transmogrifications my business with The Church of Latter-Day Eugencis are brewing in me. He twists his face, labours over a thought. Dares to reveal an old Irish secret.

"Fulton, if I tell you something can you keep it to yourself? This isn't a joke. Twenty-five years must count for something, right?"

"I think it does."

He looks into my eyes, and scopes out what I have, till now, been reluctant to describe as my swelling inner effeminacy. Fulty-poo.

"Thing is, I'd rather tell you than those Luddite coppers in my precinct."

"So fire away." I almost add, "Sweetie."

"My last wife Marge, I think I mentioned her before."

"She's wife number two?"

"The very same. A real man-hating bunny boiler, dunno what I was thinking. Young and foolish I suppose. Anyway . . . she castrated me."

"I know the feeling. Oh, how I kno-o-o—"

"Only, you don't," he replies so offhandedly that I begin to feel a bit more confident about quelling this ebb and flow of gashiness. "Course, there was a time when Marge appeared to be the perfect spouse. The first six months were virtually hassle free, hardly marital bliss but nice, yano? Then she caught me with a copy of BIG COCKS IN TIGHT CLUNJ and she, well . . . "

"She scalded you for it, destroyed the last shred of your dwindling masculinity, then left you a veritable eunuch?"

"You're half right pal. C'mere."

O'Donoughie leads me to the gent's bathroom. I follow him because my journalistic instincts are tingling, I'm about to see something unusual. Inside the bathroom, O'Donoughie checks beneath the cubicle doors to make sure we're alone.

"What's this about? You show me yours so I show you mine?"

"I told you this wasn't funny, Fulton."

"Sorry . . . "

"I got nothin' to show."

O'Donoughie unzips his trousers and peels them to the knee revealing his groin area. I'm staring at a bald, smooth stump of bone instead of a copper's grizzly old cock.

"Marge really did castrate me. Now I'm not even a man."

"Christ, Bill . . . "

***

"Make it happen," is editor code for "make it up if you have to."

We find a gaunt and haunted-looking Joe Nicoleaky flanked between the Shoreditch literati in a bookstore called The Haggerston Clique that used to be an old warehouse. The sound of everyone tapping away on their laptop keyboards sounds like metal spiders scurrying across linoleum, and instantly gets on my nerves. Nicoleaky

sits there in a bespoke couch drenched in natural light—the She-God illuminating his presence among the other drones. He sees us coming and cowers. I tell him to relax, we mean him no harm.

"You scared me!"

Already he seems like a shadow of his former self.

"You're lucky that's all we did. How was your hallucination?"

"My . . . ? You did drug me?"

"Course we did," says Cheryl.

"Well, if you must know, I visited the boudoir of a beautiful negress, whose hair was set in cornrow coils, her tits were two great saddlebags of dark meat . . . her pussy . . . "

"Alright mate, you're embarrassing my intern."

"It was like nothing I've ever experienced."

Nicoleaky is rubbing the nut of bone on the limp of his wrist, all shy-like. I can't stop thinking about O'Donoughie and his smoothie. I bet the poor castrato sees Marge every time he closes his eyes, every time he gets a phantom pang in his loins.

"All I can feel is love these days, why is that? I don't know what to do with myself."

For once in her life, my sidekick is rendered speechless. This new Nicoleaky is too much of a non sequitur for her. Having gained sustenance from conflict his whole life, now, suddenly, the berk "doesn't know what to do with himself." I suppose we're not so dissimilar he and I. The only difference is that I grew sick of the conflict a long time ago. Nicoleaky had to be drained like a cyst of his hate and anger.

"I don't even want to hang around the university anymore. Just want to look after them, make them a hot meal and instil a sense of compassion in their hearts."

"You finally grown out of chasing schoolies?"

"I suppose so. I was worried you were conducting some kind of witch hunt against me."

"Can I be honest, mate?"

Nicoleaky nods.

"I kind of was. Or I wanted to, at least."

"And now?"

"It's gone. Just the same way it seems to have left you. All that hatred. Feels like it evaporated. I'm just tired now."

"You still remember your journalistic code of ethics?"

"Got it memorised:

Truthfulness, accuracy, objectivity, impartiality, fairness and public accountability—as these apply to the acquisition of newsworthy information and its subsequent dissemination to the public.

"As I say, I ain't interested in moral turpitude anymore."

"Finally, the custodians of democracy come to the fore!"

"Finally."

"A hungry man is an angry man. A hungry journalist is a dangerous person."

"Well I guess I'm not a journalist anymore. Time to apply for a job at *The Guardian.*"

***

The sound of Galway crystal bells clanging causes everyone in the streets to clutch their ears in a chorus of agony, the shattered spiral of cochlea popping like the air-filled hemispheres of bubble wrap beneath the faint pressure of eager fingertips, is almost as majestic as horrific. I couldn't Adam and Eve it.

I lied before when I said my name was Fulton. I am currently occupying the person of Fulton, but my real name is . . . well, it's not important what my real name is. I can't remember what I used to be, I only know that journalism is the first rough draft of history, and that it was my calling. Because I altered my personality so many times I have a tendency to forget certain details about my past—not that they're relevant anymore. I am almost certain I was a woman, certainly "a woman trapped in a man's body," as the people I once dismissed, dissed and libeled as "buggerstuffing pansies" like to say. But, in a sense, I know only Fulton. I realise this must sound bloody odd to you but I ask you to reserve judgment—you have never lived in this place, though most of you have never been deprived of the basic necessities I have been deprived of. The only company I have is my own, so I will squat inside this singular body with multiple people. I don't feel the need to hide behind this Hackney hack . . .

I am not crazy. I am very rational—it's rational to want to stave off ridicule by teasing out new and exciting companionship from deep within, isn't it? I have some semblance of a "self." Other characters and personalities live inside me, but there is one brain, one will! I'm in a "fortunate" position where I have enough time to myself that I can let these people out from their synaptic corridors, free to roam and develop inside the same fleshy vessel. Blindness is the selfish man's burden. He knows it could be worse, but yearns for the full sensory experience.

In other words, I have achieved beatitude.

***

The Galway crystal bells cease. This is our call to prayer. We head for The Clit.

The back room turns out to be a downright ballroom. Simply draw aside the "wall of purple cloth" that Cheryl observed when she was infiltrating this place. All along it's been a temple veil, like the one in wicked geezer Herod's big town hall, that split and tore apart when Jee-zus gave up the ghost on the Roman gallows.

This big curtain is all sexy dark-purple, and thickly embroidered with the same ripped-off Freemason squiggles that scar our bodies. It's pulled aside on holy occasions like this, opening up like a big vay-jay the hole that resulted when the Ipsissimettes broke down the partition between this and the other half of the building, an abandoned rope-making warehouse dating back to Sheila's salad days as an embodied Victorian slum girl. And now we have a spacious venue for a Cecil B. DeMille-type mob scene!

Bryan Fix and the other alley-lurking victims have emerged from shameful shadows and blissful backyards all over Hackney, and shown up here to get group-married. It's the happiest hallelujah-howling climax in all of literature! Life is affirmed, with an exploding grin on its broad kisser. Nicoleaky is here, too, amongst the procession, a broad smile on his face. Swathes of eyeliner make his peepers pop.

Along with their gametes, all have shed their shitty personalities, myself included, as we mob the ballroom. Fix is no longer the reality TV twat; Nicoleaky has become colorblind as any upper-middle-class liberal; the female MP for Hackney North and Stoke Newington has stopped being whatever kind of political arsehole she was prior to Blue Lotus and her truck with the She-God (whatever that might have entailed). And, as for me? Apparently I can produce actual textbook-qullity full English stools these days. I go blissfully in and out of the unisex potty, right next door to the gas ring altar.

75

Everybody now has more or less identical, easygoing personalities, the same generosity of spirit I recognized in High Priestess Susanna, the cashier, and the Ipsissimette staff of the dildo and porn store, just on the other side of that door. Our reproductive abilities, such as they were, seem to have been the source of our generalized arseholism in the first place.

Not only personalities and gender, but racial characteristics have amelioratred to a mildly happy medium. Everyone's cafe-au-lait—or perhaps lait-au-cafe. There's nobody here but us hexadecaroons, with our caramel frappuccino irises, nary a pale penis to bring us shame.

And, along with our pigmentation, our scars, too, have taken on the appearance of increased niceness. No more scary alchemical hieroglyphs or Masonic fetish-sigils. Pretty little kitschy floral smoochies decorate us, in pastel colors. They could be merely henna and cartoony decals, washable-off with tears of squealy joy.

Nicoleaky, now looking and sounding just like that dead pop star from America (forgot his name) who was *really* nice to boy-children, steps up and trills in alto range the story of his depoliticizing encounter with the big Afro-Mammy in the smog. Everyone breaks down in tears, myself included.

We have become Latter-Day—not *Saints* (though we are every bit as saintly as those creatures wearing pastel bathrobes on papist holy cards)—but Latter-Day *Eugenicists*, and we wear nothing but glowing white undergarments.

Welcome to our mass wedding!

It does my heart good to see everyone gathered together in blissful pairs. It is simply *gorgeous* for this book you're holding in your hands to end in such utter sweetness! There isn't a lot of "utter sweetness" going around these days, is there now? I still can't remember who I really am, but Fulton can finally rest in the dark recesses, like bollocks retracted into unmuscled tummies. He was so-o-o-o tired!

There are same-sex, different-sex and indeterminate couplings, with the beautiful white lacy wedding dresses on men, women, hermaphrodites, transsexuals and undecideds.

Our female MP for Hackney North and Stoke Newington is circulating among the congregation with one of those trays slung around her shoulders, the type of rig worn by cigarette girls in dance halls in the thirties—except, no tobacco for us splinter-Mormons. No, she's laden with free liberal government handout sandwiches, intended for anyone who looks a bit peckish—which is nobody, for we are all floating in a state of blissed fulfillment! Hers is a ceremonial function.

Outside the venue a pink and turquoise schoolbus is parked, full of blond, blue-eyed, perfectly Aryan kids, each plump and glowing, as in a classic Nazi propaganda pamphlet. On the side is painted—

OPTIMAL TODDLER ADOPTIONS DOT COM

They were recommended by a certain fabulous, sparkly, giant creature, an adoptive parent, who will regale us with his/her presence tonight, right here in front of our faces. Among the happy couples he/she/it magnificently swaggers-swishes-sashays: yes, it's the "man" formerly known as Bill O'Donoughie, CID. He now goes by the assumed title—

MISS CATAMENIANA,
the six-foot-ten *autogynephiliac*!

That big-arse word appears stitched in contrasting-colored sequins across her bosom. And it now appears on the style sheet of the scandal rag from which I have recently resigned. Another neologism, coined by us, the rank and file of the Church of Latter-Day Eugenics, has also made it onto *The Prattler*'s style sheet. It's what our Asian English major Ipsissimette would call a "portmanteau term," and is particularly useful on this joyous day. It's an amalgamation of the outdated pronouns *She* and *He*, tied off at the end with an unapologetic *It*.

Henceforth, *Prattler* articles will refer to us as *Sshee-it*.

The Ipsissimettes tried to save me and Cheryl from this former O'Donoughie by sacrificing *ssheeit*, but found out, the hard way, that *ssheeit* was already a eunuch. No fluids to harvest. They wound up cherishing *ssheeit* as an earthly manifestation of the god/goddess Hermaphrodite, like in Fellini's *Satyricon*, which I've never seen,

but read a Wikipedia article because, back when I was Fulton, I once tried to bone an educated tart.

So, O'Donoughie was repressing all this lack and sad news in his trousers, a mean cop, until *ssheeit*'s pants were pulled down and *ssheeit* got loved for *ssheeit*'s true secret self. *Ssheeit* has blossomed, like Elton John, quit *ssheeit*'s job and become the mascot of the dildo store, a magnificent cock queen.

"O'Donoughie looks so beautiful," Cheryl says with genuine affection (but politically incorrect terminology), as Miss Catameniana appears from behind the door to The Clit. Our cheers bring tears to my former intern's eyes.

Yes, Jocelyn and Evelyn's adopted pater is the celebrant of this sacrament, the priest-priestess who conducts the ceremony, a perfect dream in a golden lamé form-fitting full-length gown that shows her celestial tits and fourteen-inch long tickle-gizzard to advantage (it seems, oddly, to have grown in the same afternoon she was ordained): the personification of perfect, transformative, strictly unproductive fucking; she is the She-God's representative on Earth, and everyone is dazzled.

Cheryl's positioned right in front of him/her. The girl's been promoted to the position at *The Prattler* recently vacated by me, and is here to cover the event of the Hackney social season. She's interviewing La Catameniana, in true *Prattler* style—

"So, you lot are poofters, innit?"

I can see the headline tomorrow:

THE LATE REVEREND SUN MYUNG MOON'S UNIFICATION CHURCH TAKES A PAGE OUT OF THE YANKS' BIBLE, DECREES MASS POOFTER WEDDINGS IN HACKNEY!

Busloads of underage Sting-clones
are parked outside the venue,
to service full-tilt buggerstuffery pedo-orgies
at the reception, subsequent
to the appalling sacrilegious rites!

I've mentored my sprog well. Tears of pride well up and dribble down my cheeks, leaving rivulet trails in the tastefully thin layer of Revlon's new foundation product, *Caramel Frappe*, "Designed with the discerning hexadecaroonette in mind!" also doubling as a sunscreen.

And a good thing, too, for the She-God, way upstairs there, in response to this happiest of all endings, opens up the sky, and all of London lights up like the Bahamas! Old Sol/Sal (androgynous now) shines on La Catameniana's hubcap-sized sequins, and everyone is dazzled to helpless, blind ecstasy. Moderately severe sunburns all round!

Am I surprised? Of course I'm not surprised. Since just before the turn of the millennium, my soon-to-be former employer has reported breathlessly, weekly, on this simultaneous emasculating-defeminizing trend in major western industrialized blah-blah. (I forgot to ask Sheila in the Smog with Garments how long ago Big 'n Hung dispatched her back here to her hometown.)

So, have I not given to you the happiest ending of any book ever written, with an entire London bourough redeemed in the sunshine? I know this is how the world should be, because Fulton is finally quiet, the bristly brute.

Not that the hangovers and full English diarrhoea will necessarily change—just my method of dealing with them. For the former, I'll be visiting a boutique in Mayfair for a proper naturally annealing herbal balm to swathe my throbbing brow. As for the latter, somehow, I have a feeling I'll be wiping more daintily 'round my rim, and opening the window rather than exposing Cheryl to what, apologetically yet somewhat preciously, I'll call *the miasma*—which, in any case, I suspect, won't smell nearly as bad from now on. It will waft of fresh *biscuits*, as the American Mormons call them, or *dinner rolls*, as they are known this side of the pond. My asexually reproduced creation will be firm, cylindrical, with spiral grooves, and tapered toward the swirly tip, just like the St. Mary Axe skyscraper that Sheila abuses as a sybian, only caramel-cream colored.

Bushels of Tampax, sheafs of Kotex and liters of substandard sperm are being dumped and poured on a bonfire in the middle of the ballroom. As Brother Brigham once promised—

the smoke thereof ascends to heaven as an offering . . .
and this incense atones!

We join hands to sing The She-Hymn—

Sheila, our mum since ages past,
Our mum for years to come!
Our shelter from the stormy blast
Of thy terrific bum!

Our chrism is the monthly clot,
Our spunk the leavened loaf!
By rental are our kids begot!
Our labia are scrotes!

Sheila, recline on Hoxton smog!
Receive your snack of smoke
From wanky Yanks, exotic wogs,
And reg'lar British blokes!

Tomorrow I've a job interview at *The Guardian*. And some of my haikus are being "seriously considered" by a kindly young editorial assistant at *Granta*.

About the Authors

Chris Kelso is an award winning genre writer, editor and illustrator from Scotland. His short stories and articles have appeared in magazines and journals across the UK, US and Canada. *Unger House Radicals* won the Ginger Nuts of Horror Book of the Year in 2016 and *The Black Dog Eats the City* was featured in the Weird Fiction Review's best of 2014.

Tom Bradley has published twenty-five volumes of poetry, fiction, essays and screenplays with houses in the USA, England, Canada and Japan. Various of his novels have been nominated for the Editor's Book Award, the New York University Bobst Prize, and the AWP Series. *3:AM Magazine* gave him their Nonfiction Book of the Year Award in 2007 and 2009, and one of his latest graphic novels is excerpted in last year's & *Now Award Anthology*. His journalism and criticism have appeared in such publications as Salon.com, and are frequently featured in *Arts & Letters Daily*.

About the Illustrator

Nick Patterson works mostly with black ink to illustrate surreal and often nightmarish scenes. Occasional acrylic paintings interrupt his practice with aggressive brushwork and the opportunistic use of vivid colours. He combines the fluid motion of Frank Frazetta's drawings, the monstrous sexuality of H.R. Giger's paintings, and the enigmatic dream-like quality of David Lynch's films. Through an eclectic range of subjects, Patterson's work seeks to baffle its audience while engaging a sense of visual pleasure to hold the viewer's gaze. He lives on the west coast of Canada and is currently studying in Visual Arts.

Boiled Americans by Michael Allen Rose

Boiled Americans is a puzzle box in book form, inspired by the violence of living in urban America and exploding the tendency to forget or ignore.

Great American Slasher by David C. Hayes

Baseball, apple pie . . . and murder.

The Bohemian Guide to Monogamy
by Andrew Armacost

Here, a strange labyrinth of interlinked short fiction assembles itself into a darkly moving novella that deftly explores the bottomless pain and pleasure of love and commitment, the hinterland between youth and adulthood.

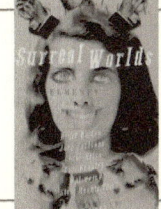

Surreal Worlds edited by Sean Leonard

An anthology of surrealistic compositions created by some of the finest names in genre fiction. A showcase of international talent undaunted by the conventions of language and common narrative structures. Here is timelessness. Here is Surreal Worlds

How to Succesfully Kidnap Strangers
by Max Booth III

Do not respond to bad reviews. If you must respond to bad reviews, please do not kidnap the reviewer.

ADHD Vampire by Matthew Vaughn

He came, he conquered, he was distracted a lot

Notes from the Guts of a Hippo
by Grant Wamack

A rugged journalist travels to Brazil in search of a missing hippo researcher and the notes left behind lead to something earth shatteringly revelatory.

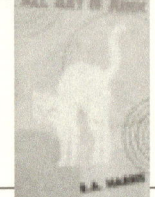

All Art is Junk by R. A. Harris

Lana Rivers, a girl with paintbrush hair, is missing and it's up to Lancelot, her cyborg knight, and his bionic conjoined twin, Cilia, to find her before her evil father, a disrespected artist turned mad-scientist, performs a terrible experiment on her.

Cherub by David C. Hayes

Cherub wasn't like the other boys—too slow, too rough—but he didn't deserve what that hospital did to him, and now he will make them pay.

Skinners by Adam Millard

Los Angeles, the City of Angels. At least, that's what the brochure says. What it fails to mention is the earthquakes. Oh, and the flesh-eating creatures lying dormant beneath the concrete, waiting for the chance to surface once again. Their wait is over . . .

The After-Life Story of Pork Knuckles Malone by MP Johnson

What's a farm boy to do when his pet pig becomes an evil, decaying hunk of ham with slime-spewing psychic powers?

A Lightbulb's Lament by Grant Wamack

A gentleman with a lightbulb for head wakes up in a world full of darkness, hooks up with a beautiful ex-prostitute, and an old man who can heal people; he travels down south to find the mysterious Creator.

The Horror Show by Vincenzo Bilof

A poetry novel—a narcoleptic, amnesiac Nobel Prize-winning poet becomes the subject of an experiment to cure madness.

Beyond by Jordan Krall

From Jerusalem to Mars, psychiatry and the unraveling of the universe

Gravity Comics Massacre
by Vincenzo Bilof

An absolutely shitty novella involving comic books, aliens, a serial killer, teenagers in an abandoned town, horror-trope dream sequences, and an ending you're going to hate.

Glue by Scott Lange

Sticky bowels and sticky situations.

Ascent by Matthew Bialer

Is the 8 foot tall creature haunting a small town in Iowa in the fall of the year 1903 the product of a hoax and collective imagination or was it one of the first documented paranormal event in America? This epic poem grapples with these questions.

Elusive Plato by Rhys Hughes

The last in a long decadent line of piratical Spanish eccentrics, Bartleby Cadiz grows up in isolation to be as mad, bad and metaphysical as his ancestors. But he feels there is something different about him. What can it be?

The Fairy Princess of Trains
by Christopher Boyle

Danny's mediocre life turns upside-down when his couch starts whispering to him. Then he's charged with a supernatural mission: Rescue the Fairy Princess of Trains.

Terence, Mephisto & Viscera Eyes
by Chris Kelso

9 new science fiction stories from Chris Kelso

Industrial Carpet Drag by Bruce Taylor

Chemicals make you do great things!

Bizarro Bizarro: An Anthology

The finest bizarro short stories from 2013.

Necrosaurus Rex by Nicolas Day

Necrosaurus Rex tells the tale of Martin, a simple janitor, who takes an unfortunate trip through time, becomes a violent mutant, and the father of us all. There's 14 billion years crushed inside these pages, and most of them are pretty nasty.

Day of the Milkman by S. T. Cartledge

In a world dominated by the milk industry, only one milkman survives after a terrible storm sinks all the ships and throws the Great White Sea out of balance.

Moosejaw Frontier by Chris Kelso

An unapologetic disaster of metafiction

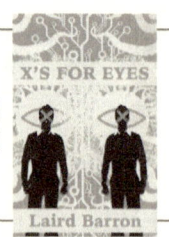

The Boy Who Loved Death by Hal Duncan

From blackest humour to bleakest horror, with twisted relish, Hal Duncan's eighteen tales dig into death—and the life that goes with it.

X's for Eyes by Laird Barron

Between the machinations of the disciples of black gods and good old corporate skullduggery, it's winding up to be of a hell of a summer vacation for the Tooms Brothers.

Omega Grey by Seb Doubinsky

When professor Todd Bailer embarked on a psychedelics quest to discover if the land of the Dead really existed, he had no idea he would threaten the cosmic balance of the universe by triggering a real-estate conquest of the new Frontier.

Berzerkoids by MP Johnson

The first short story collection from Wonderland Book Award-winning author MP Johnson

Retch by David Bernstein

What would you do if you were cursed to puke right before you reached orgasm? You'd do anything, right? (You know you would.) Find out what one wealthy, good-looking, playboy will do to try to end his abhorrent curse.

Static/Orgone by Jamie Grefe

A double-novella of literary grindhouse nightmares and theoretical post-apocalyptic vengeance.

Wonder Weavers by Matthew Bialer

An epic poem about a mysterious sighting in 1896.

Battering the Stem by Bob Freville

A darkly comic urban crime novella. What would it take to make you beg?

Cartoons in the Suicide Forest by Leza Cantoral

When we're dead
You know she'll adore us